"I know you have your own life in Dallas."

Max rested his forehead on hers, then backed away completely, as if realizing he just couldn't get that close.

Dallas. Yes.

The fog cleared, and snatches of life—real life—pressed back to the surface. But she didn't want real life. She wanted to stay in this pocket of stillness. Where there was only the twinkle of the stars and the love in a certain cowboy's eyes and the whisper that life—her life—could still be different. Could be restored.

"But maybe…" Max's voice trailed, and he tucked a wisp of hair behind her ear. "Maybe."

Maybe. So much potential in that word. So much hope. When was the last time she'd hoped? She wanted to hope. Wanted to feel again. To believe. To trust. Was it possible?

"Maybe." She breathed out the word. *Maybe* would have to be enough for now.

Maybe would hold back real life a little while longer.

Books by Betsy St. Amant

Love Inspired

Return to Love
A Valentine's Wish
Rodeo Sweetheart
Fireman Dad
Her Family Wish
The Rancher Next Door
The Rancher's Secret Son

BETSY ST. AMANT

loves polka-dot shoes, chocolate and sharing the good news of God's grace through her novels. She has a bachelor's degree in Christian communications from Louisiana Baptist University and is actively pursuing a career in inspirational writing. Betsy resides in northern Louisiana with her husband and daughter and enjoys reading, kickboxing and spending quality time with her family.

The Rancher's Secret Son

Betsy St. Amant

HHARLEQUIN® LOVE INSPIRED®

Recycling programs
for this product may
not exist in your area.

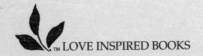 ™ LOVE INSPIRED BOOKS

ISBN-13: 978-0-373-81742-9

THE RANCHER'S SECRET SON

www.Harlequin.com

Printed in U.S.A.

And we know that all things work together for good to them that love God, to them who are the called according to His purpose.

—*Romans* 8:28

To my Best Friend, Jesus Christ,
whose sustaining presence was with me during
the writing of this novel in a way like never before.
I can do nothing apart from you! I love you.

Chapter One

Despite its name, Camp Hope didn't manage to lift Emma Shaver's spirits. If anything, she just felt heavier.

She leaned over the steering wheel of her SUV as they rolled nearer the camp, ignoring the steady thump of her thirteen-year-old son Cody's fingers pounding a rhythm on the dashboard beside her. The camp's main structure, a two-story, log cabin–style house, held court in the middle of autumn-weary acreage, still dry from the unforgiving heat of a Louisiana summer, faded golden fields stretching as far as the eye could see. The outbuildings, a rustic, get-it-done crimson barn and an open-sided lean-to, nestled behind two rows of temporary buildings that, according to the camp's website, served as the dorms for the teenagers.

Cody could probably weasel his way out of one of those with a toothpick.

Rat tattat.

She inhaled a tight breath. Pick her battles, was her motto. Cody was here, ready—if not willing—to get the help he needed or else. That was a battle she had to fight. Annoying drumbeats were not.

Rat tat tattat.

Camp Hope looked tired. Or maybe she was just tired.

Rat tattat.

"That's really getting old, Cody." So was the headache pounding at her temples that hadn't stopped since their appearance in court. The day she got the news that would forever change her world.

Again.

Cody shrugged and flopped against the seat, the seat belt stretching across his thin chest and tangling in the cords of his iPod. At least he'd changed shirts. That was yet another battle she'd had to fight this morning before driving to Broken Bend, Louisiana. She wasn't sure where he'd gotten that holey, rumpled excuse for a T-shirt, but she knew enough about gangs to know it was going straight into the trash.

Too bad all her psych books didn't tell what to do when the client was your own kid. The rules blurred then, the text grew fuzzy. Nothing was black-and-white anymore like it used to be in college when she'd been working toward her degree. She might have earned her master's and opened a successful clinic in Dallas, Texas, against all odds, but at home—she was an epic failure.

But she wouldn't cry. Not in front of her son.

She steeled her nerves. "We're here." Not exactly the way she imagined her Monday going, but hey, life was full of surprises. She could write the book on that one.

Cody yanked the iPod buds from his ears, grumbling. "I still don't see why I had to come."

That was precisely the problem. She counted to ten before answering, even as she steered the car toward the dusty, gravel parking lot. "You heard what the judge said. It's either Camp Hope or juvenile detention." She pulled into a spot between a beat-up pickup and a shiny hybrid. Guess it took all types to have troubled teens. Yet the reminder didn't make her feel better. This wasn't anyone's kid—it was *her* kid.

She angled a glance at her muttering son as she shifted into park. "You think me making you change shirts was bad? At least it wasn't an orange jumpsuit."

Cody snorted, but she could tell her point got across. He grudgingly released his seat belt and peered out the window at the house before him. Was he as nervous as she was? It was hard to trust a system she knew from her job didn't always bring positive results. But the judge had been adamant, and here they were. It beat juvenile detention by far. Apparently the facility had become quite popular with local officials for its moral-based program and positive outcomes.

She'd have been more prone to hope except the camp was back in her hometown—the town she hadn't visited once since her father's funeral five years ago. She'd arranged to take some time off and stay with her mom in Broken Bend while Cody went through the program, maybe work on some of her own issues. She couldn't avoid her hometown forever, and Cody would benefit from seeing his grandmother again. Besides, despite her own painful past, she had to do what was best for her son. Being nearby if he had a breakthrough was crucial. He'd been miles away for far too long already.

But what if the camp didn't help and Cody ended up in juvie later anyway?

Her stomach flipped, and bile rose in her throat. Here she was a professional counselor, and her son had been caught breaking and entering into his school and vandalizing the gym with a crowd of older teens—after shoplifting the month before and getting into a fistfight in the cafeteria three months before that.

Could one month of hard work, counseling and time spent with animals really turn him around?

Not that she had a lot of choices at the moment. She had to trust that the leaders of the program—whoever they were, as the website info had been vague at best—knew what they were doing.

Had to trust that God wouldn't give up on her son.

She opened her car door and squinted against the afternoon sunlight. Sliding her sunglasses into place, she motioned for Cody to get out of the car and grab his duffel. Packing for a month at a working ranch had been trickier than she'd thought, especially when Cody's wardrobe mostly consisted of dark pants, black T-shirts and tennis shoes. She'd bought boots after she'd browsed Camp Hope's requirements list online but couldn't for the life of her picture Cody wearing them.

Maybe that was a good thing—a sign that he would undergo a complete transformation.

She just wanted her son back. The one who used to crawl on her lap during thunderstorms, make hideouts from superhero sheets and a few chairs, and open her car door for her while boasting about being a gentleman. What had gone so wrong, so quickly?

Tears pressed behind her lids and she blinked rapidly to clear them away. Last time she'd let her guard down and cried in front of Cody, he'd snuck out of the house for three hours with no word of where he was going. Besides, it wasn't healthy for a child to see his mother cry—especially if he was the cause of the tears.

Cody shut his car door a little harder than necessary and shouldered his duffel. The defensive scowl on his face as he slipped his iPod buds back in reminded her of his dad. She'd managed to stuff away thoughts of Max Ringgold for years, until recently, when Cody's attitude mirrored his absent father's more than she wanted to admit. Cody's hair was blond like hers, but he had a similar cowlick to his dad's, a testament to their shared stubbornness. He also had that same charming, do-no-wrong smile Max had always worn as easily as his trademark leather jacket.

But Max had done wrong. A lot of wrong.

Images flashed through her mind. Weapons stashed under truck seats. Rolled up baggies of white powder stuffed in the glove box. Beefy fists banging on the window of her car, muted threats assaulting her ears as they made out down by the lake.

Yeah, once upon a time, Max Ringgold had been trouble with a capital *T.* All the more reason Cody needed help, *now*—before the darkness in his genes had a chance to fully take over.

Before she lost her son the way she'd lost his father.

A familiar finger of regret nudged her, sending an icy shiver down her back. Choosing not to tell Max she was pregnant had been the best choice at the time—make that her only choice. After she went to college and two pink lines on a stick had determined her fate, she returned to Broken Bend, panicked and unsure how he'd react. He'd made promises about his behavior before she'd left, so many promises. But a baby didn't fit into Max Ringgold's bad boy style any more than the promiscuous role she'd temporarily adopted fit into hers. Would he even accept her—*them?*

After catching Max unaware in the middle of another drug deal, with one of the county's slipperiest and most dangerous gang leaders no less, the decision was made for her. Max wouldn't get a chance to reject them.

She never looked back.

Approximately thirteen years later, Cody didn't know the difference. She'd made a home for them, a loving home, despite the sacrifices and hard work required of a single mom putting herself through college, avoiding her hometown and keeping the details a secret from her parents. She didn't want the shotgun wedding her father threatened. Not with Max Ringgold. She might deserve to pay for her mistakes, but her kid deserved better.

Yet despite all those logged miles on the treadmill, Emma had never quite been able to outrun the guilt.

She shut her car door and steered Cody toward the front porch of the main house, where she assumed registration would take place. "Let's go." Time to shake off the past—that's why they were there, after all. To get a fresh start, a second chance. Maybe for both of them. Secrets long buried were best left buried, and just because she was back in Broken Bend didn't mean they'd all be resurrected.

The front screen door squeaked open on its hinges, and boots thudded onto the wooden porch.

She glanced up at the approaching cowboy with a smile, relieved that someone was finally there to take charge. She could relax, take a much-needed break. Cody would be in good hands.

The cowboy lifted the brim of his black hat, and her smile slipped away as shock gripped her in a cold, unrelenting vice.

He'd be in Max Ringgold's hands.

Max Ringgold always figured his past would one day come back to taunt him. He just never dreamed it'd latch around his ankle and knock his feet right out from underneath him.

He stared at the blonde woman before him as if she might have two heads. Two identities, for sure, because she looked exactly like Emma Shaver. Yet there was no way. *No* way. Emma hadn't been back in Broken Bend in a decade. Maybe longer. He used to know the weeks to the day but eventually stopped counting. Hard to heal from an injury when you kept poking at the wound.

But this woman was looking at him as if he'd sprouted a second head, too—so maybe it was possible after all.

Her mouth opened and closed, then pressed into a tight line. Red dotted her cheeks. Yep, that was her. He'd always been able to make her blush. Part of the problem. He'd been inexplicably drawn to the Good Girl, her to the Bad Boy—and the chemistry that resulted could have blown a crater throughout most of the town. Why did something that happened a lifetime ago suddenly seem like yesterday?

He knew he should say something, anything, to break the awkward silence, but his years of training in dealing with troubled teens didn't cover how to deal with moms who were ex-girlfriends.

He took off his hat, then regretted it. He probably had hat hair, and now he felt even more vulnerable under her laser-sharp gaze. "I'm Max."

Emma's fair eyebrows lifted, and he winced. She knew that. But he had to say something. Besides, the kid didn't know who he was, and that's why they were there. He turned his attention to the teen standing beside Emma and offered his hand. Man to man. "Max Ringgold."

The boy grunted, reluctantly offering a quick, limp shake. They'd have to work on that. A man was known by his handshake. "Cody Shaver."

An alarm sounded in Max's subconscious. Shaver. So Emma wasn't married. He darted a glance to her left hand to make sure, and wanted to kick himself with his own boot as she caught him, well, red-handed. He slammed his hat back on his head.

"Come on inside. We'll get you signed in then catch up with the rest of the tour." Max held the door and motioned them forward. Cody clomped inside, dragging his duffel behind him on the floor. Emma followed, gaze lowered, the scent of her peppermint perfume lingering long after she squeezed past.

Max checked his watch, partly to know the time and partly to resist the urge to touch her hair, silky and shiny as a shampoo commercial—the kind that definitely didn't belong on his ranch with all the dirt, dust and horse sweat flying about. Good thing she wasn't staying.

His heart seconded that idea as she flashed wary azure eyes at him—the same eyes that peeked at him from the photo he still had stashed in his sock drawer.

The photo didn't do them justice.

He let the screen door snap behind him as he directed them to his office off the dining room, which he'd converted from an old closet. He didn't spend much time there, except for the occasional paperwork, prayer time or private conversations with the kids.

The other nine campers, three girls and six boys, had arrived and checked in half an hour before and were being given a brief tour by the live-in counselors, Luke and Nicole Erickson. He'd noticed the increasing size of Nicole's stomach beneath her maternity top earlier and had raised an eyebrow at Luke, who'd assured him she wasn't due for another month. Just in time to finish this camp. Then he'd have to find a replacement for her while she took maternity leave.

The stress of that significant problem suddenly

dimmed compared to the throbbing in his temples at Emma's proximity. He slipped behind the desk to give himself space, trying to ignore the way his heart pounded under his work shirt like a runaway horse.

"Here we are. Cody Shaver." He ran his finger over the printed name and made a check mark in the column—and a mental note not to let Nicole handle the precamp paperwork anymore. If he'd seen Emma's name as Cody's guardian on his forms earlier, he'd have had a heads-up. All he personally received was the list of the kids' names two weeks prior to camp, so he could pray for them.

Then again, the odds of another ex-girlfriend popping up seemed a little slim.

"Is there a problem?" Emma's voice sounded as strained as the muscles in his neck as he jerked his head up to look at her, realizing he'd been staring at the document for far longer than he should have. Emma Shaver. Wow. When did she have a son? How old was Cody? He'd have to check the full file later. But apparently Emma hadn't wasted a lot of time pining over Max after leaving for college.

Though she was supposed to have come back.

The thought burned his stomach and he licked his suddenly dry lips. "No, there's no problem. No problem at all." The past was the past. The important part now was that Cody was here, and he needed help—regardless of who his mother was. Max had to get his priorities in order, quick, or he'd do more harm than good. These kids counted on him, and he wouldn't let them—or God—down.

Not again.

He found his warmest smile, despite the cold expression in Emma's eyes attempting to freeze his heart. "Welcome to Camp Hope, Cody. It's going to be a great month."

The kid grunted, as if he didn't believe him. Emma didn't look as if she particularly believed him, either.

Which was fine, because at the moment, he didn't fully believe himself.

Chapter Two

Luke led the tour of the campus, the scripted words falling naturally from his mouth. Good thing, because Max was having a terrible time paying attention.

As they crossed the worn path from the dorms to the barn, Max glanced up at the white letters painted on the rustic red sign, hanging ten feet above the cattle guard at the end of his long gravel driveway. Camp Hope. He'd painted the sign himself last year, acquired three splinters trying to hang the thing and almost toppled off the ladder on his way back down. But nothing worth doing was easy, the main point he was trying to prove at his ranch for troubled teens.

He knew—he'd been one.

He shuffled behind the group of nervous parents and disgruntled teens as Luke led them into the barn, trying not to let his gaze keep resting on

Emma. But that was a little like trying not to glance at a lit candle while standing in a pitch-black room.

God, a little direction here? I'm lost. Max was confident he'd followed the Lord's guiding when he opened Camp Hope over a year ago and received the training necessary to minister to teenagers. He'd already watched almost seventy teens graduate the month-long program, many of whom had come to know God in the process. For a lot of them, Camp Hope was the last stop before juvenile detention, or worse. Max knew how to smell contraband cigarette smoke a mile away, knew the current gang loyalty colors, and now, after trial and error, knew the vents in the dorm could be pried open and made into a hiding spot.

He just didn't know how to look at Emma Shaver without bursting into flame.

Max rested his back against the door frame of the barn and inhaled the comforting aroma of horses. One by one, the teens perked up as Luke went over the rules of horsemanship and what chores would be expected of them in the stables. Funny how they'd give endless grief over making their beds, but most had no trouble shoveling manure or grooming a colt. Something about horses reached deep inside and brought out the good in folks.

A stirring of anticipation returned, and Max fought to hold on to it. He'd been so excited about this particular camp a few weeks ago as the planning process wrapped up. Somehow, he just knew this session would be the best one yet. He felt it in his spirit during his morning Bible readings in the sunroom, heard it in the excitement in his own voice when he shared his plans with his best friend and former boss, Brady McCollough.

Brady had just slapped his hat against his leg to free it of dirt, and heartily agreed. He could feel it, too, and Max trusted his friend's judgment. Brady lived several miles down the road, but the back of their two properties joined at a barbed wire fence. Max had saved for years to be able to buy one hundred acres near his friend and finally start his own spread. Brady's wife, Caley, said he and Brady argued more than an old married couple, but that was just because they knew each other so well and remained friends anyway. Max had been there for Brady through the tragic death of his first wife, while Brady had been responsible for hauling Max out of the muck and into a church pew. If Brady felt that same prompting, Max could bank on it.

It was just that so far, he didn't have a clue how Emma Shaver and her kid showing up at his camp could possibly be a God thing. Maybe more like a cosmic joke.

Brady would definitely get a kick out of this one. Would probably rattle something off about God working in mysterious ways. Max usually agreed— but this went a little beyond mysterious. Still, he'd do his best to help Cody like he would any other teen there, and thankfully would have little to do with Emma. After all, it wasn't Cody's fault Max knew his mom from another lifetime ago. He refused to let that fact filter through in any of his interactions with Cody. Another month and Emma would be right back out of his life forever.

Apparently like she'd always wanted.

"And that's the tour." Luke clapped his hands, jerking Max back to reality and causing two boys to jump. "Boss?"

His mind raced. He really had to get it together or he wouldn't be a very good example. He took a deep breath and tried to center his head on anything other than Emma. Tour over. So, time for dinner. Then the inevitable parent-teen goodbyes, which was his least favorite part of the camp. He shot a glance at Emma. But today, that part might be a good thing.

He found his smile and gestured toward the main house. "Time for grub, everyone!"

A few teens murmured their pleasure; others kept their hollow expressions as they filed out of the barn and toward the house like a chain gang. Max fought a grin. The campers always started out the same, and with God's grace, usually ended with an 180-degree change. Hopefully this session wouldn't be an exception. It just took faith, perseverance— and a huge dose of patience.

He ended up at the back of the line, Luke in the lead, with Cody lagging in the middle. The humid Louisiana wind ruffled Max's hair and loosened

the crowd. "Just so you know, I'm taking a leave of absence from work and staying at my mom's while Cody is here. I wanted to be nearby—just in case."

Max frowned. Just in case what? She changed her mind about the camp? Or was she that worried about Cody making it through the program? So many questions. Yet only one escaped his mouth. "What do you do?" It'd been years since he'd looked her up on the internet, at the start of the social media hype, but her pages were all set to private. Not surprising. Even less surprising—he didn't have any of those pages for himself.

She shot him a look he couldn't quite interpret, her voice lowering to a near whisper. "I'm a child psychologist in Dallas."

He almost snorted. Child psychologist. And yet Cody… He didn't have to state the obvious. If Emma was anything like he'd remembered, she'd probably beaten herself up about that enough. She was good at emotional pummeling.

Just ask his heart.

Max Ringgold had done well for himself. Emma almost didn't even recognize the muscular, smiling cowboy that had greeted her and Cody on the front porch and now sat across from her at the dinner table. Hard to reconcile this Max with the one she'd known years ago, as a naive teenager about to head for college. That'd been a daredevil, moody, flirty Max. This was a successful Max. A contented, living-for-a-purpose, fulfilled Max.

Scared her to death.

The shock that had racked her body when he lifted that hat brim earlier had almost knocked her in the dirt. How did someone like Max come to lead a camp for troubled teens? He *was* a troubled teen. Apparently he was drawing water from the "been there, done that" well. Had he really transformed so completely? It seemed that way.

Yet for all his success, there was something in his eyes when he looked at her that didn't seem all that complete.

She knew the feeling.

She winced as Cody stabbed at the green beans on his plate with more force than necessary. The campers and parents were sharing dinner together in the main house before the adults left for the night. During their tour, she'd seen a large working kitchen with a temporary live-in cook Max affectionately dubbed Mama Jeanie, a dining room with a picnic bench–style, carved wooden table big enough for everyone to eat together, and a bathroom that surprisingly smelled like peaches and cinnamon. Max's quarters were upstairs, the only part of the house he deemed permanently off-limits.

To the back of the dining hall was a room with a locked door, which Max and the other counselor Luke let everyone peek into briefly—the recreation center. Treadmills, an old-fashioned Pac-Man arcade game, an air hockey table and a large-screen TV with different game systems were just a few of the treats she glimpsed before Max shut the door, explaining the rec room was incentive and a reward for good behavior, only. That is, the kids had to earn it.

Emma liked this setup already, though she could tell by the tight line of Cody's mouth he didn't necessarily agree.

She tried to send him a silent warning with her eyes as he continued to scrape his fork against his plate, forming a rhythm he nodded his head to. The dark-haired teen sitting to his right immediately picked up the grunge-band sound, tapping his knife against the side of his half-empty water glass and stomping his foot under the table. An older teen girl with blond curls snorted and rolled her eyes at them.

"Cody."

He ignored her, as usual, and the parents continued to eat as if nothing had changed, as if their ears weren't suffering from the high-pitched screeching sounds. Maybe that was part of why their kids were there in the first place. Did their efforts to be noticed always go ignored? Not acknowledging cries for attention wasn't always the best course of action. They weren't innocent toddlers playing the drop-the-spoon-from-the-highchair game. They were miniature adults who needed positive reinforcement—and consequences for negative behavior.

Well, these parents might think ignorance was bliss, but she wasn't that kind of mom. *"Hey!"*

She looked over in surprise as her firm voice mixed with Max's gruffer tone. They'd spoken at the same time. He glanced at her, amusement flickering in his caramel-colored eyes, then back to the kids.

"All right. That's enough." His deep voice left no room for argument, and if that hadn't been enough, the I-mean-business glare he turned on them would have been. He was establishing his authority from the beginning, a smart move. Max had common sense after all. Maybe Cody would be fine here.

As long as they didn't discover the truth before she was ready.

The weight of her secret pressed her into her chair, threatening to send her crashing through the raised floorboards and landing somewhere in the basement below. How low could she sink? Even a tornado cellar didn't feel far enough, deep enough, dark enough to conceal a secret of this magnitude.

Thirteen years of getting over Max Ringgold, of convincing her heart he didn't exist, and now he was in charge of her son for a month. No, *his* son.

God really did have a sense of humor.

She realized she'd been staring aimlessly at her plate and quickly sat up straight and brushed her hair off her shoulders. Thankfully, Cody had stopped his impromptu band immediately, and the other kids had followed suit. One grumbled incoherently, but Max let that go. So he picked his battles, too, didn't demand perfection.

Really weird they had that, of all things, in common.

Was it possible this was part of God's plan for Cody? Maybe this was the avenue he needed to turn his life around. God knew what He was doing... right?

Emma sure hoped someone did, because she'd never felt more lost. How embarrassing was it for her to struggle to understand her own child, when she was paid good money to evaluate the inner musings of other kids? In all her career, she never imagined she'd end up here.

Probably just part of the punishment for her own reckless choices that summer. Wasn't there something in the Bible about the sins of the fathers affecting their children? And speaking of fathers and sins...she kept her eyes lowered as she studied Max. He looked more like Cody—or rather, Cody looked more like him—than she'd realized at first glance in the parking lot. The way they hunched over their plates, one forearm resting casually to the side, was identical.

Hopefully no one else noticed the similarities. Her stomach hurt just imagining that particular scenario. At least Cody would have no reason to suspect. All she'd ever told him growing up was that his father had been a bad guy who left her when she was pregnant. Not a complete lie—even though she'd been the one to technically do the leaving.

But Max had left emotionally first when he chose to do that drug deal and break his promise.

She sat back, pushing food around her plate with her fork as she observed the way Max interacted with the other parents. Patience personified, though he didn't seem patronizing or condescending. Just confident. The parents, especially the mothers, seemed to warm to his personality like butter melting on a crescent roll. Not flirty, though one father did scoot his chair closer to his wife when she laughed at something Max said.

She swallowed a sip of water, her appetite long diminished from the tension-laced drive over with Cody and the surprise of seeing Max again for the first time in so long. Her body hadn't caught up to her emotions.

And if her stomach kept jumping every time Max's gaze flitted her direction, it might not ever catch up. Over a decade had passed, and he still had the power to physically undo her.

She was absolutely terrified to analyze that one.

"Well, folks." Max scooted his chair back with a scrape against the polished wooden floors and stood. He braced his hands on the table, leaning forward slightly and pausing to briefly look every parent in the eye. "It's time to say goodbye. I've learned the hard way already that here at Camp Hope, dragging it out isn't good for anyone."

No kidding. She'd end up crying and Cody would end up looking for an escape. Not like he needed any more prompting to run away. It wouldn't be the first time. She slowly stood with the others, fighting the rising panic welling in her throat as they filed outside to the porch. He would be fine. And so would she.

But what if he found out? What if Max found out?

She smiled at her son, who bobbed his head in a nod but didn't return the smile. He was nervous. She could tell by the pinched brow and the way his bottom lip curved on the side. Suddenly, all she could see was her baby boy, the one who used to follow her around the house, zooming a fire truck under her feet and burning his fingers on the cookie sheet because he was too impatient to wait. He needed her. Needed his mom.

But the only way for her to be there for him now was to leave.

Unwanted tears welled, and she blinked rapidly, forcing her voice to stay strong. She held out her arms, praying he would pacify her request for a hug. He fell quickly into her embrace, then hid a sniff behind a cough. She clutched him tightly, despite his stiffening against her touch, and tuned out the sounds of the parents around her performing similar rituals with their own kids.

Far too soon, she pulled away until she could see Cody's eyes. "I'll be back when it's time. You just obey Mr. Ringgold." The name tasted foreign on her lips, but her heart knew it well.

"He said to call him Max." Cody kept his eyes focused somewhere past her shoulder, and she could only assume it was for the same reason she kept darting her gaze to his nose. Easier not to cry that way. Maybe he wasn't so tough after all.

She pulled him in for one more hug, despite his grumbled protest. *Don't overdo it, Emma.* But the self-coaching wasn't working. Her desperate mommy heart kept taking charge. "Just obey. Let's do this right and get you home, okay?" She still couldn't believe she was telling anyone to do what Max Ringgold told them. Once upon a time that would have been a prison sentence—or worse.

"I know." Impatience crowded Cody's tone as he pulled away, and she bit back any more natural but unwanted advice. He was about to get plenty of that. Maybe he'd listen to someone else. But Max? It went against every instinct she had.

Still, he'd proved himself at the dinner table with the kids. He was capable and in charge. Max wasn't a punk teenager anymore, and she wasn't a needy girl attempting to fill herself with the temporal.

Mostly.

She grazed Cody's arm. "You know I love you, right?" She couldn't help it—her voice cracked.

"I know." Cody shuffled his feet, nodding with a jerk. "Relax, Mom. I'm not a murderer or anything."

At least there was that. She figured she wasn't

getting a return "I love you," but then again, he hadn't said that in a long time. Probably not since she got him his iPod at his last birthday.

She forced the negative thought away. They were here. They'd get through this, and she'd figure out what—if anything—to do about Max later.

Her eyes darted to where he stood a respectful distance away from the group, giving the parents space to say their goodbyes, and then flicked to the ground as his gaze met hers. Right now, her secret was safe, and Cody was in a good position to do what he needed to do. That was what mattered the most. The rest would just have to wait.

Max would just have to wait.

Chapter Three

Emma poured herself what had to be her fourth cup of tea in the past two hours—and still, her headache had yet to abandon ship. She settled back against the throw pillows on her mother's couch, then adjusted positions as a knotted tassel dug into her spine. She'd hated those pillows growing up. Still did.

Her mom sat across the coffee table from her in a straight-back chair, one sandal-clad foot bouncing an easy rhythm over her crossed leg. Her softly curled brown hair was cut the same, maybe a little shorter. The wrinkles under her eyes were new. Then again, the bags under Emma's eyes were relatively new as well, thanks to Cody.

"Camp Hope is a quality facility, Emma. Cody will be fine." Her mother paused as she took a sip from her teacup. "It will be good for him to get out of Dallas for a while."

"I know. You're right." But she heard what her

mom wasn't saying. *You should have brought him here more often.* And maybe she should have. But she'd made her choices, and they worked for them. Or at least, they had worked until Cody cannon-balled off the deep end.

Besides, it wasn't as if she kept Cody from his grandmother. Her mom came and stayed with them in the city multiple times during the year, shopping, dining out and enjoying spa days at Emma's expense. She didn't mind pampering her mother—her father never did growing up, and her mom definitely deserved it.

Mom just never understood why Emma kept her secrets to herself.

"Will you still be in town for Thanksgiving?" Her mother's tone was even, controlled, so much so that Emma couldn't decipher the meaning behind the words. Did she want them to stay? Was that hope hidden? Or resignation of the inevitable inconvenience?

"I guess it depends on the program and Cody's graduation." She rolled in her lip. Thanksgiving. Seemed aeons away, though it was only about a month. "If Cody graduates then we should be able to join you. Or you could follow us to Dallas and we could get together there." If he didn't graduate… then Cody would go to juvie? Would the judge give him another chance? Would Cody stay out of trouble long enough to make it through the holidays?

She'd heard the tone of voice the judge had used

when he'd pulled her aside privately after the hearing. "I know this is hard on you," he'd said. "Especially as a counselor. So I'm playing this straight with you—Camp Hope is Cody's last chance before serious repercussions. He's on a bad road, Ms. Shaver, and the people he's keeping company with are on a worse one."

Like she didn't already know.

But hearing it from an official's mouth, from someone who had the authority to put her son in some form of teen confinement, made the slap of reality sting all the more.

Cody *had* to get through this program.

Emma set her teacup on the coffee table, emotion clogging her throat, and stood as her mother wisely remained silent. Adrenaline raced against exhaustion in a never-ending marathon. This was so messed up. She should be planning what to get her son for Christmas, not wondering if he'd even be home on December 25.

She moved to the lace-covered front window, admiring the sunset and soaking in the peace it offered as she ran her fingers over the worn edges of the curtains. They hadn't changed, either. But then again, her mom didn't have any more money now than she did when Daddy was alive.

She closed her eyes, breathing in the musty, familiar smell of the house of her childhood. She hadn't been home since the funeral a few years ago. Even then, she'd kept to herself, rigid in the corner with a sandwich tray, feigning a smile and hoping Broken Bend didn't stain her any further than it already had. She'd left after convincing her mom to come stay with them in Dallas. She had—and after two weeks' worth of facials, manicures and new outfits, her mother went home.

While Emma went back to doing what she did best—fixing everyone else's kids.

"We need dessert." The chair squeaked as her mom stood. "You want a cookie? Homemade oat-meal raisin."

She'd barely touched her dinner at the ranch, but comfort food sounded good. She accepted the plate her mother brought back from the kitchen and plucked a cookie from the top. Crumbly, just the way she liked them. She settled back on the couch, catching the crumbs with her hand. "You always made the best cookies, Mom."

She smiled at the compliment. "You look like you need about ten more of them. I thought Dallas had all the best restaurants."

"It does. We love eating out in the city. It's just…" Just what? She was too stressed lately to eat? Too consumed with Cody's issues to take care of herself? She wasn't avoiding food. It just seemed so irrelevant compared to the bigger things going on in their life.

She intentionally took another cookie. "The campers and parents all ate together at Camp Hope earlier. I was really impressed with the way Max handled himself." Shocked, too, but that detail wasn't worth mentioning.

Her mother bit into her cookie, dusting crumbs from her pants onto the floor. "It wasn't awkward, then?"

A raisin stuck in her throat, and Emma coughed, half choking as the raisin made a painful descent. "No—no, why would it be?" Did she know? After all this time, all the planning, all the carefully laid out details, her mother *knew?*

"Didn't you hang out with him in high school a few times? When you were friends with what's-her-name...Laura. That Laura girl, with the hair that came all the way to her bottom end." Her mom gestured with her cookie.

Laura. The friend she used as an excuse when she decided to go out with Max. Emma winced. Laura existed, but the friendship wasn't nearly what she'd implied back then. She couldn't lie now—but she couldn't totally evade the question, either, or her mom would grow even more curious.

She sipped her tea until her throat stopped burning from the coughing fit, then set the cup casually back on the table. "Yeah, I know Max. But it wasn't awkward." Awkward didn't even begin to cut it.

Her mom tilted her head. "I wonder what happened to Laura. She seemed like a good kid. Maybe a little misguided, though."

Good grief. Emma's parents had been more sheltered than she thought. She knew she'd covered her tracks during her rebellious streak after senior year, but she hadn't known she'd been *that* good. Laura was never without a cigarette in hand, even in the Broken Bend Church of Grace parking lot, and the stories of Laura's weekend activities filled the chairs at the hair salon more than once. But that's what happened when your father was a deacon and your mother taught Sunday school—not a lot of privacy, and a whole heap of judgment. Emma never knew for sure how she managed to get away with such a friend, but when compared to Max, Laura was a downright goody-goody.

"I think she moved away." Like they all had, with their heads lowered in shame. Except for Max. Of all of them that hung out together that fateful summer, Max had been the one to stay and shape up his life. Talk about ironic.

She shifted uncomfortably on the couch. She couldn't let the same thing happen to Cody, couldn't let a season of bad choices ruin his life—or at least alter it forever. She couldn't honestly say her own scarlet letter had *ruined* her life, but it'd definitely changed it. And left a permanent mark.

Cody deserved better. He had to take control now, before things spiraled out of everyone's control. The judge was giving him a second chance at the right path, and if he didn't take it, they'd all be roaming in the wilderness.

She couldn't do that again—even if she deserved it.

Her mom sighed and ran her finger over the handle of her teacup. "I'll never understand why you all wanted to get out of Broken Bend so badly. There's something to be said for home, you know."

Emma smiled and nodded, ignoring the tassel once again poking her in the back. Yes, there was.

But there was a lot more to be said for leaving.

Max hadn't felt the urge to leave in a long time. But watching Nicole double over with her second contraction in the past two minutes made him want to turn his back on Broken Bend and bolt for the hills.

She turned wary eyes on him, as if somehow this whole situation were his fault, and braced both hands against her back. The morning sun shining behind her through the open barn doors served as a spotlight for her distorted silhouette. "Don't even say it."

"I wasn't going to say anything." Max didn't know much about expectant women, but he knew enough to be quiet. About, well, everything—especially the particularly bad timing of this event. He was supposed to have a month—four weeks. An entire camp. This changed everything.

What was he going to do?

But it changed a lot more for Nicole, so he wouldn't dare address it. He took two steps backward, out of the barn. So much for their morning trail ride. "I'll get Luke."

"I'm here." Luke rushed up behind him, boots clomping on the dirt-packed floor, sending several horses jerking their heads in aggravation at the interruption. "I was just getting the horses saddled outside when Stacy told me what happened." He rushed to Nicole's side. "Are you okay?"

"I'm having a baby. I'm great." She wiped tears from the corners of her eyes, laughed and then winced as what had to be another contraction crumpled her expression. "No. Not great. They're getting closer together, and stronger."

"So, I guess we're not going riding."

Max turned. Stacy, his oldest camper, a seventeen-year-old with curly blond hair, crossed her arms in the center of the barn aisle. The question in her voice held more than a bit of amusement, and even a punch of satisfaction. Something along the tune of *I dare you to try to fix me now. You can't even run your own camp.*

He'd heard that tone before, and there was only one solution. Denial. "Of course we're still going riding." He cleared his throat and lowered his voice an octave to show authority. "Luke will take Nicole to the hospital, and we'll saddle up as planned. Tell the others."

Stacy rolled her eyes but thankfully turned to obey.

Good enough for now. One hormonal woman at a time, and the one standing in front of him took first priority. He focused on Nicole, who was still alternating deep breaths with winces of pain as she waddled toward the back door of the barn—the one closest to the female dorms.

It was official. He was about to be one chaperone short of a camp. And with his other counselor, Faith, working only part-time since she had young children of her own, he now had no one to stay overnight with the female campers.

God, I need a plan here. And uh, Nicole needs a doctor. Looked like her baby would be four weeks early, unless they were able to stop the labor at the hospital. And even then, he knew enough to understand she'd likely be on full bed rest until the baby came. He swallowed his dismay. "You want me to call 9-1-1?"

Luke stopped as he caught up to Nicole and turned, shaking his head. "Her suitcase is ready. We'll just grab it and head that way. I'll call you if we need anything." He started to say more, then stopped as Nicole clutched his arm. "See you later, man." He ushered her away, and just like that, Max was left in a bind.

He breathed a prayer for safety for the baby and Nicole both, added one for sanity for Luke, and then headed into the sunlight to face ten campers.

Alone.

Make that another prayer of sanity for himself.

He forced a smile and took a deep breath as he faced his campers, some standing with concerned expressions, others feigning—or perhaps truly feeling—disinterest.

"So there's been some excitement here on your first day." He laughed, then cut it short when it sounded as awkward as it felt. "Nicole will be— uh, indisposed—for the rest of this camp session. For good reason, of course. I know she wishes she could be here with you guys. And girls."

Great. Now he was stumbling all over himself, and the kids just stared at him, expecting answers, and he had none to give. He rolled in his lower lip. "Don't worry, I'm working on a replacement now." Or at least, he hoped God was, because he had zero ideas. Luke and Nicole had been his right hands bringing this camp together the past year, and now he was short. Leaving him handicapped and near panic.

His mind raced. He still had Faith, who would be there later that afternoon; Tim, the middle-aged chaplain who also acted as dorm leader and could stay with the guys overnight; and two college kids who served as activity chaperones as needed on a part-time basis. He could see if they'd offer a few more hours, maybe bribe them with gift cards to stay the night here and there to assist Tim. And if Nicole was able to stay on bed rest, then maybe Luke would still come do a few stints as much as he could until she actually had the baby.

He nodded slowly, trying not to panic. He could do this—but not without another female counselor.

Someone from the church, maybe? They'd be willing to volunteer, at least, for the ministry angle. But who was qualified to do it? He didn't just need a babysitter, he needed someone who could interact with these kids and *reach* them. Someone like Luke and Tim, who understood the guys, knew how to talk to them. Could love them without letting them get away with stuff.

His eyes landed on Cody, who seemed to be avoiding what was going on as he rubbed a black mare under her chin. Mental note—the boy liked animals. Just like Emma always had. He wondered briefly what other interests he shared with his mom—

Emma.

He swallowed as an idea lodged in his mind and refused to budge. Emma, with her child psychology degree. Emma, who was staying nearby at her mother's and had nothing to do until Cody graduated the camp in a month.

Emma, who'd been the only other person at the table to speak up during the teens' impromptu concert and showed ability to handle this group of unpredictable, miniature adults.

No. He couldn't.

But as his eyes swept across his three female campers and landed on Stacy's pointed smirk, resignation took over any lingering trace of pride. He had to ask her. There was no one else available on such short notice, certainly not anyone qualified.

She could still keep her space from Cody since the majority of their activities were gender-separated. The first day trail ride was an exception, to get all the curious boy-girl stares out of each other's systems. He'd make sure Cody didn't feel smothered having Emma on the grounds.

But would she do it?

And could he really ask her?

"The details will work themselves out. I'll get someone in here ASAP. For now, let's go ahead and saddle up." Max clapped his hands together, sending a few teens scurrying for their mounts and the others groaning and eyeing their horses with dismay. He knew the feeling. He pretty much wanted to moan and pout, too. *God, I know this camp was Your idea, so I'm hoping You have a plan here.*

His sinking heart confirmed what he knew and didn't want to admit. God had a plan, all right.

He just really wished it weren't going to have to involve Emma Shaver.

Chapter Four

Emma swung on her mom's front porch swing the next afternoon, her bare feet pushing off the wooden deck. Clanging dishes sounded through the screen door, where her mother was cleaning up from lunch, erasing all evidence of their chicken salad sandwiches. She'd offered to help, but Mom insisted Emma stay outside and enjoy the afternoon.

Sort of how she'd insisted she do the laundry that morning without help. And cleaned the kitchen last night after their snack without help.

Day two, and already Emma wondered if her welcome was fading. That was her mom, though, especially since she became a widow—routine, routine, routine. And Emma wasn't fitting inside it. Maybe that answered her question about Thanksgiving.

She sighed. Could they really make this last a month without driving each other crazy? They had a temporary routine figured out when Mom visited them in Dallas. Everyone had their own room, their own space. They kept a busy schedule so they wouldn't be on top of each other all day. Home, however, was a different story.

Did she really just think of Broken Bend as home?

She didn't want to go there.

Emma tilted her face to the sunlight streaming across her lap and released a deep breath, trying to erase the tension of the past forty-eight-plus hours. The verdict at court. Seeing Max, leaving Cody. The secrets, the burden. She still had to figure out what to tell Max, and when.

Later looked pretty appealing.

She closed her eyes, letting the warmth of the October afternoon sink into her skin. This entire situation left a bad taste in her mouth, and it had nothing to do with the fact her mom had used a little too much mayo in the salad. Her past had caught up to her—and not only caught up, but taken over. She had to deal with it. But what was best for Cody right now?

Tires crunched gravel and she opened her eyes to see a red, extended cab truck pulling into the drive. She squinted at the driver, drenched in shadows as he exited the vehicle. Surely her mother didn't have male visitors… No.

It was Max.

They really had to stop meeting like this.

"What'd he do?" The question sprang from her lips and carried across the yard before she realized how heavy it sounded. Heavy with fear, with accusation. With expectation of failure. How ugly of her. She swallowed the rest of it, clamping her teeth on her lower lip. Max being here didn't automatically mean bad news.

But it probably didn't mean good.

"Hey." Max took the steps in a single hop and came to face her, pausing to remove his hat. His brown hair wilted across his forehead and he shoved it back before replacing what she always thought of as his natural appendage. Max always had two arms, two legs and a hat. Some things never changed.

And some things did.

"Did something happen?" She crossed her arms over her chest, willing away the heartbroken girl from thirteen years ago that rose inside, urging her to run to the safety of her room and lock the door. Shut him out. Convince herself she hadn't made a mistake and wasn't making another one by trusting her son to Max's supposed expertise.

But the professional adult stood her ground and forced what she hoped was a natural-looking smile. At least forming her fears as a generic question made them sound more approachable. Less assuming.

"Happen to who? Cody?" Surprise lifted Max's brows. He shook his head, and relief melted her from the inside out. If Cody got kicked out of the program…

"Sorry. I didn't think how my showing up would seem." He did look sorry as he adjusted his hat for the second time. Worry wrinkled the skin above his nose, and his smile faded to a half quirk. "I didn't mean to scare you."

"It's okay, I wasn't scared." Terrified was more like it. The adrenaline abandoned her limbs, and she sank back on the porch swing. "Just concerned."

"Cody's fine. Doing great." Max edged closer to the swing, though he chose to lean against the porch rail instead of join her. Which was as he should. She wouldn't remember the times they'd sat on that same swing well after midnight, while her parents were asleep, and laughed. Whispered. Kissed.

Wouldn't remember that at all.

"We took a trail ride this morning, and now the campers are having a rest time in their room before we introduce them to barn chores." Max shook his head, as if he realized he'd been stalling. "That's not why I came, though, obviously. I had a question, and it wasn't one to ask on the phone."

Nerves twisted her stomach, and she gripped the rusty chain of the swing. Surely he hadn't come for her. To talk about the past. What if he'd somehow noticed how similar he and Cody—

"I need help."

The blatant admission took her off guard, and

she snapped her gaze to meet his. "With what?"
Max Ringgold never needed anyone. Except maybe
his dealer, back in the day. He'd made that clear
more than once. He didn't need family. God. Her.

Maybe some things had changed since then, but
how much could a person really transform?

He tucked his thumbs in the front pockets of his
jeans, another signature Max move that threatened
to sweep her back in time. She kept her gaze riveted
to his, determined to ignore the memories desperate for review. She was here for Cody. *Her* son. Not
for some traumatic, tormenting stroll down best-
left-forgotten lane.

She straightened slightly, steeling herself for his
request. Whatever it was, she had no obligation to
answer. He would treat Cody—and her—like any
other camper or parent on the ranch. Just because
they had a past didn't mean she owed him a thing.

"My lead female counselor went into early labor."

Well that wasn't what she expected. She frowned.

"Nicole will obviously be gone the rest of the
camp, whether she has the baby early or not. And
that leaves me shorthanded with the men, but completely—well, unhanded I guess you'd say—for the
girls." Max let out a slow breath. "So, I was thinking…with your degree, and all, with counseling,
you said…that…"

Oh, no. *No.* She knew what he wanted now, despite the fact he didn't seem able to get the words
out. And with good reason. Of course she'd say no.

"No."

He didn't seem to hear, just took the spot next to her on the swing. She shifted automatically, hating the alertness that rushed her senses at his proximity. If she'd heeded those warning signs thirteen years ago…but no. Cody wasn't a burden. He was a gift. Even now, through this struggle. He was the best part of her life.

And the most painful.

"Emma, there's no one else."

"In this entire world?" She was exaggerating, a telltale sign of panic and loss of control, but she couldn't help it. She couldn't do this. Not for myriad reasons, namely her secret. Even now she felt it bubbling within, churning her insides like a cauldron of lies. But it wasn't her fault. She'd done what was best for her son. Mothers protected their children.

Even from cowboys.

"Well, sure, there's probably someone even right here in Broken Bend, but not right now. Not qualified. Not sitting on their mother's porch with nothing to do for a month." He gestured to the house, and suddenly she was embarrassed over its chipped, faded condition. What was wrong with her, still caring what Max Ringgold thought all this time later? "The girls at the camp need someone they can talk to. I don't just need a chaperone in the dorms at night or another body on the trail rides. I need someone I can trust with them."

"Trust *me?* I'm the mother of one of your campers." *And you're the father.* The words practically burned her lips. "No. You don't want me."

Not the words she meant to use. Her cheeks flushed, and she looked away, across the yard, staring at his red truck until her vision blurred. "I mean, I'm clearly not much help."

"You're still a professional." Max pushed the swing off with his boots, and the gentle breeze stirred by the sudden motion cooled her heated face. "I'm sure it's different when it's your own child acting out, anyway. Hasn't someone told you that?"

Of course they had—everyone in her clinic had for that matter—but that didn't mean she believed them. Or that they were right. She shook her head. "What about Cody? I don't need to be there, cramping his style or getting in his way. He has to come first."

"The boys and girls typically keep separate schedules, besides mealtimes. I'll make sure he doesn't see you more than necessary." Max's eyes tried to draw her in, and she pointedly looked away, though there was no avoiding the familiar scent of his cologne. "He'll know you're there, of course—I won't lie to him. But it won't be a problem."

It was actually starting to make sense. That was the scary part. Emma shook her head again, though she didn't know why. She couldn't actually do this. But hadn't she just been wondering how she and her mother would make it through the month? Still, awkwardness for a few weeks was a thousand times better than keeping her mouth shut around Max for that long.

"Please, Emma. You're here. You're available." He paused, and she risked a glance. He was frowning as if hit with a sudden thought. "You are available. Aren't you?"

Now. Here it was—her out. But no, she was completely, totally available. With zero reason to turn this opportunity down other than the one reason she couldn't reveal. Her secret. Hadn't she chosen this profession to help others? What would happen if she turned her back—would Max have to send the female campers home? Then what—juvie? Jail? Probation? House arrest? They deserved more than those options.

Because Cody deserved more than those options.

She pressed her lips together, unable to believe she was even considering this. "You can't pay me. It'd seem unethical given my relationship to an existing camper."

Max held up both hands in surrender, grinning as if he knew he had her. But then again, he'd always known. That was the problem. "Not an issue there, trust me. The extended staff is volunteer, anyway."

Volunteer. Right. Volunteer to put herself in Max's presence every day, ministering to kids she wasn't worthy of teaching. Qualified, sure—but not worthy. Not with her own failures slapping her in the face every time the police showed up with Cody. Every time the phone rang with another telling of his misadventures. Every time he smarted off to her and snuck out of the house.

But if she didn't offer what little she had, who would? Were the girls better off without her? She thought back to the list of "or else" options the judge had provided Cody and shook her head. No, she was the lesser of those evils for sure. Everyone deserved a second chance.

"So? What do you think?"

Well, maybe not everyone. She darted a glance at Max, at his hopeful mask permanently pressed in place, then at her mother's silhouette in the kitchen, obviously listening to their every word. She pressed her lips together to hold in her sigh and nodded before she could talk herself out of it. "I'm available. I'll do it."

She might be available. But when it came to Max Ringgold, her heart was one hundred percent obligated elsewhere.

That hadn't been as hard as he thought. Well, in some ways, maybe harder.

Max drove slowly away from Emma, refusing the urge to stare in his rearview mirror at her reflection still settled on the porch. Sitting next to Emma on the swing had been a blast from his past he'd never dreamed of reliving. Well, he'd *dreamt* of it all right—memories that refused to die, visiting him in his sleep—but he never imagined he'd actually be there again in person.

Though this time she'd squeezed as far away from him as possible. Definitely not like the last time they'd swung on her parents' front porch, late at night while her parents slept, Emma tucked under his arm so closely that he barely had to move his head to plant a kiss on her strawberry-scented hair.

Max tightened his grip on the steering wheel. Those days were gone. Emma had obviously moved on since then, having a kid with someone who apparently wasn't in the picture anymore. That was too bad for Cody, though he had to admit—deep down, he was a little relieved Emma was single. Clearly she'd been with another man at some point in her life, but at least he didn't have to see the guy who'd stolen the only woman he'd ever loved.

But now he had to see her every day for a month.

He pulled back into the ranch drive a few minutes later and stopped to send a few quick text messages to his team members about the temporary change in staff. Thankfully Faith, his part-time worker, had agreed to stay the night instead of leaving after dinner as was her usual routine. She could supervise the girl campers until Emma arrived the next day.

Less than twenty-four hours.

He hit Send on a group text and tossed his phone on the seat beside him, pausing to take a deep breath and focus. Reset his mind away from Emma and back on his duties. Rest period would be about over by now, so it'd be time to introduce the kids to barn chores. Some of the teens would have never held a pitchfork in their life—never lifted so much as a finger, for that matter, toward real labor. Other kids in this camp probably had worked so hard as children because of their family's financial circumstances, they'd been worn down and burned-out by age fourteen or fifteen. There were always different reasons for the rebel heart.

For him, it'd been a matter of history repeating itself.

He slammed the truck door shut just as Brady rode up the drive on his favorite horse, Nugget. Oh, man, Brady would have a time of it hearing Emma was back in town. After all the teasing he'd doled out to Brady a few years ago about his wife, Caley, when they were dating, Max would be in for an earful. He'd wait a bit, make sure the timing was right before telling him—and make sure Cody wasn't nearby. The last thing the kid needed was to discover his temporary guardian had a history with his mom.

This was getting a little more complicated than he'd realized. No wonder Emma had been so hesitant to take the job. Still, it had to be done.

A quick glance confirmed the ranch was quiet, the barn not yet teeming with the afternoon activities. He probably only had a few minutes before the counselors rounded up the teens and brought them out.

Max squinted up at Brady against the afternoon sun, grinning as Nugget stomped and snorted beneath his friend. "Cut it out, Nugget. You're not so tough." He reached up and rubbed the horse under his mane. "I've seen you run away from a bull."

Brady swung easily from the saddle, the leather creaking beneath his displaced weight. "Yeah, I saw it a little too closely. From the ground up."

"Not that you're holding a grudge against me for being gone that time Spitfire got out or anything." He crossed his arms and attempted a stern expression, but it was hard not to laugh at the story that never got old—Brady being chased across his pasture by an ornery bull who'd escaped his pen a few years ago.

"Actually, no. Not bitter at all." Brady gathered Nugget's reins over his head and looped them in his fist. "That was one of the things that brought me and Caley together."

Max grinned. "Then you're welcome."

Brady shoved Max's shoulder, and he laughed as they led Nugget toward the barn. "What brings you by, besides boasting about your marital bliss?"

"Not boasting. Just appreciating." Brady tugged at Nugget's reins to prevent him from nibbling the grass near the red structure. "Though I do hate to admit when you're right."

"Get used to it, pal." Despite all his teasing along

the way, Max had encouraged Brady, a former widower, to act on his feelings toward Caley when she'd worked as his daughter's nanny. "Caley still volunteering at the fire department?"

Brady nodded. "Only when they get overworked, or when there's a big fire."

"So only during the times it would make you the most nervous."

His friend rolled his eyes with a groan. "Pretty much. But it's working out. She's good at what she does."

"No doubt." Max looked again toward the dorms, halfway eager to tell Brady what had transpired in the past two days, and halfway dreading it. Though he'd never met her, Brady knew the whole story about Emma—the whirlwind relationship, the way Max fell faster than a steer during a team roping competition. Her desertion. If anyone would "get it," it'd be his friend.

But admitting he was still so affected by her didn't come naturally.

"I actually came to borrow your wire puller." Brady gestured toward the general direction of his property. "Have a fence to repair and Ava broke mine last time I let her help." He cut his eyes at Max. "And trust me, I say *help* lightly."

Max snorted. But Brady was letting his young teen daughter, who he'd kept on a tight leash since her mother's death years ago, spread her wings on the ranch, and for Brady, that was huge. Another hats off to Caley there. "Sure, no problem. It's in the barn." Finding the puller would give him more time to decide how to break the news of Emma's return—and that she had a son—to his friend.

And time to figure out how to say it in a way that wouldn't put Brady on the alert to Max's not-so-dormant feelings for her.

Brady tied Nugget's reins to the hitching post and Max led the way inside, blinking to adjust his eyes to the dimmer light. He opened the supply room door. "Here it is." The wire puller lay on the top shelf, just where it should be. He never imagined in his years of working for Brady that one day he'd have his own spread—and that it would be organized, no less.

"Top shelf. I trained you well." Brady helped himself to the tool and stepped back, grinning as he shut the door. "Seriously man, this is awesome what you've got going here. As much as I hated to lose your help at the Double C, you've done well."

"You gonna need a tissue?" Max joked, but the compliment sank in deep. Praise from Brady always meant a lot. They'd seen each other through some rough times.

Hopefully that wasn't an omen of what was coming along with Emma.

Brady clapped his shoulder as he passed him in the aisle. "Maybe marriage made me a little soft, but whatever. I still recommend it."

"I hear you." They walked in silence back toward

Nugget. Max was running out of time to talk before the teens descended on the barn. It was now or never. He drew a deep breath, fighting to keep his voice casual. "So, turns out Nicole went into labor a little early. Guess who's filling in with the female campers?" Not that Brady could ever actually guess.

"Someone from church?" Brady turned at Nugget's side and handed Max the wire puller so he could mount.

"Not exactly." He hesitated. "Someone who recently came back to town."

Brady's brows lifted. "I'd guess one of your exes, but there's too many to keep up with all their geographical locations."

Max passed the puller to Brady in the saddle. "Ha-ha-ha, very funny." Yet true. So what if Max had dated a lot—or more than a lot—back in the day? Including the local veterinarian, which hadn't gone over well with Brady when Max had been in his employ. It didn't matter—he wasn't like that now, despite his former reputation. Besides, all those women had just proved one fact to him over and over again.

They weren't Emma Shaver.

"So it's not an ex." Brady gathered the reins and turned Nugget toward the road.

Max rolled in his bottom lip, stepping back to give the horse room. "I didn't say that."

"I really need to get this fence repaired, man.

What's with the guessing game?" Brady shifted his hat back on his head as he peered down at Max. Nugget snorted his own impatience, and Brady's eyes slowly narrowed. "Unless it's—"

Gravel crunched as an SUV parked a few yards from where they stood. Brady's head swiveled to look just as Max recognized the vehicle. Emma was early. They'd agreed for her to show up first thing the next morning, Wednesday, yet here she was. And from the way she grudgingly heaved her suitcase from the backseat and blew her hair out of her eyes, she was tired. Maybe even grumpy.

This wasn't good. He hadn't had a chance to talk to Cody or do more than text the other counselors the news of the fill-in help. Hadn't had a chance to tell Brady the turn of events.

Hadn't had a chance to wall up what was left of his heart.

"I'm here." Emma set her wheeled suitcase on the dusty ground at her feet, looking as if she thought simply being there would have to be enough. Good thing Max had turned off the idea of more a long time ago. Somewhere around the time she disappeared from his life, maybe. But no, it'd taken a lot longer than that.

Still was taking time, if he were painfully honest.

He shot a glance at Brady and let out a long sigh. The inevitable had arrived, right on time. "Welcome back." He focused his smile on Emma, hoping he successfully hid the nerves wringing his stomach. "This is Brady, a neighbor and friend. And, Brady, this is the temporary counselor I was telling you about—Emma." He swallowed, darting a glance as Brady automatically reached down a hand to shake hers. "Emma Shaver."

Chapter Five

Emma had no idea why Max's friend Brady seemed to lose his tan right before her eyes when they were introduced. Or why his friendly grip on her hand seized up like a vice.

She pulled it free and fought the urge to rub off the lingering pressure. "Nice to meet you." Mostly, anyway. She shot Max a quizzical look, but he was staring at Brady beneath the rim of his cowboy hat, as if waiting for a bigger reaction. Suddenly she got it.

Brady knew about her. About her and Max.

Her face flamed and she reached down to pick up her suitcase. She'd been through enough the past few months—standing here like a circus sideshow wasn't going to be next on her list. "Sorry I'm early, just needed to go ahead and get settled." And get away from her mother's prying, never ending questions before the truth erupted from her soul like a jet stream. "I'll just get out of your way, as soon as you tell me where to unpack." Too bad that couldn't be back in Dallas. But no, she was here for Cody. And now these female campers.

Definitely not for anything else.

"No problem. The female dorms are there, and the girls are probably finishing up their rest time. Faith's in there." Max pointed to the temporary building behind the barn. "I make a point not to go inside those dorms, to avoid any negative appearances. But once you go through the front door, you'll be standing in an entryway. Bedrooms are to the left, bathrooms to the right."

"I'm sure I can figure it out from there." Anything to leave the awkwardness hanging in the air like a noose. Yet whose neck it was destined for, she wasn't sure.

She adjusted her grip on her suitcase and risked another glance at Brady, who finally had the decency to look away and pretend as if he hadn't been staring. Though *staring* was putting it mildly. He ogled as though she might have just arrived from six feet under instead of via a used SUV.

What exactly had Max told his best friend? And why did it matter a decade later?

Refusing to ponder either question any further, she began to roll her suitcase toward the dorm, but Max interrupted. "Brady was just leaving. Broken fences wait for no man. Right?"

Emma caught the look he shot his friend, and Brady immediately caught on.

"Right, right. The fence." Brady held up the tool in his hand and forced a laugh. "Duty calls." He glanced at Max, then back at Emma as he proceeded to urge his horse forward. "Nice to, ah, meet you, Emma." He started to say more, then shook his head and rode away, dirt stirring beneath his horse's hooves.

She raised an eyebrow at Max. "That was subtle." The guy who'd stolen her heart along with a variety of goods from the Broken Bend General Store once had apparently lost his ability to be sneaky.

He rubbed his jaw, either hiding a smile or he'd acquired a new nervous tick since they'd last parted. "He had a fence situation."

"And a staring problem."

Max snorted. "He was surprised to see you, that's all. Sort of like—"

"You were?"

"Trust me, Brady's a good guy. The one responsible for, well…" He held out both arms to his sides. "Me."

There were so many potential sarcastic responses to that, she wasn't even sure where to start. She opened her mouth then shut it. She wasn't that girl anymore, and Max wasn't that guy. Being snippy wouldn't solve anything but prove her master's degree didn't make her as mature as she'd thought. Stress didn't give her the right to be rude. She was better than that.

Most days.

He shot her a knowing smile. "Dinner's at six in the main house." He hooked one finger through the belt loop of his jeans, projecting a confidence his tone didn't complement. Did her sudden appearance this afternoon throw him off as much as seeing him had startled her yesterday? She should have kept to the plan to come tomorrow. But her mom…

Emma blew out her breath. "I'll be there." She paused, manners taking over—partly from years of training and counseling, and partly from guilt over the mental debate she'd just processed. "Do you need anything before then?" *Please no, please no.* She needed space. Time to debrief. Time to figure out how she was going to put up a wall thick enough to keep Max and the memories at bay, while allowing the girls she was in charge of access. They'd see right through the facade. She had to be real and honest with them in order for any progress to be made in their lives.

But Max didn't get that privilege.

And who was she to assume he'd even want it?

Her pulse pounded in her temples, and a dull headache began to creep down her neck and into her tight shoulder muscles. She reached up to rub it.

"No, dinner is fine." Max shifted his weight, his body language a telltale giveaway of how uncomfortable he felt around her. Well, that made two of them. "That gives me time to get the kids settled into barn chores this afternoon and explain to Cody your presence here. Hopefully before he sees you."

Cody. Her heart twisted as the headache roared to a full blaze. "I didn't think about how you hadn't had a chance to warn him yet." Though everything else she'd have to eventually tell Cody paled in comparison to this. She briefly squeezed her eyes shut and opened them to find Max's face lit with concern.

"You all right?"

"Just a headache. Been getting them a lot lately." Oops. She hadn't meant to reveal that part. She didn't want Max's worry, and she knew the headaches were only because of stress and her own inability to handle everything. She had to get it together. For Cody's sake, and for her own. She wasn't useful to anyone like this. How would it look if she not only failed with her own son, but with the girls at this camp, too? No, she had to prove she could overcome.

Prove that she was enough.

"There's some pain meds in the main house if you'd like some Tylenol." Max's forehead crinkled as he studied her, his cocoa eyes bright and piercing beneath his hat. He'd always been able to see too much. That was part of why she refused to lay her sights on him again after her decision to leave had been made.

He'd have read—and changed—her mind.

She looked away. "I've got medicine in my bag." She never traveled without it anymore these days, considering the frequency of her headaches.

"That's fine, but if it's anything stronger than Tylenol, I'd prefer you lock it in the medicine cabinet in the house." Max gestured toward the dorms. "So it's not a temptation for the campers."

He was right. She needed to get her head in the game. Though the reference to drug use rang some sort of ironic bell. Did he even remember all that he'd put her through? No doubt Max had come a long way from his past.

But if that was true, why did it still feel like yesterday?

She swallowed the memories and accusations daring to burst free and nodded briefly. "No problem." Once she steeled her heart, she met his gaze and boldly held it, hoping to be dismissed. Until Max's expression softened completely off cue.

"I'm really glad you're here, Emma."

A warning sounded deep in her stomach, and she drew a breath so fast and tight her chest hurt. She squeezed the handle of her suitcase to hide her suddenly shaky hands. He said that as if he meant it. As if maybe the past decade wasn't so far away for him, either.

Max's eyes widened. "You know, as a counselor. It's a big help."

Right. The camp. Her breath released from her body in a sudden whoosh of air, and she steadied herself with her suitcase. Who was she fooling? Besides, she had no doubt he'd take back the sentiment if he knew exactly who he was in Cody's life—and that the role went a lot deeper than counselor at a therapeutic camp.

If the secrets she accused Max of having in the past were bad, what exactly did that make hers?

Guilt tied her quivering emotions into a tangled knot, and for a brash moment, she considered blurting it out. All of it. She could get her whole point across in about two questions. *Remember that night after the party on the Bayou, when you told me you were a different man because of me? Well, do you care to guess when Cody's birthday is?*

What would happen if he knew? Right now, before anyone got any deeper into this mess? Would he send Cody home? Would it be considered too close of a conflict for him to stay?

Would Cody have a chance elsewhere?

She wanted the best for her son, which is why she booted Max out of their lives in the first place. But how could she keep digesting this secret for a month without completely self-destructing?

Suddenly, the door to the girls dorm opened, temporarily solving her dilemma. Three teens piled outside into the afternoon sunshine, followed by a woman who looked to be in her mid-twenties, shiny brown hair pulled up high in a ponytail. She wore a whistle around her neck and a smile that made even Emma want to confide in her.

"There's Faith, now. She's great and will be here helping you out as much as her part-time schedule allows."

Emma nodded, though she wasn't sure which burned worse. His compliments and obvious admiration of Faith—or the fact that she even noticed.

"The campers are Stacy—" Max pointed discreetly to the older, curly-haired blonde Emma remembered from dinner the night before "—Katie and Tonya. Katie's the short one, and Tonya is the tall one. Stacy is seventeen, Katie and Tonya are fifteen. They're both from Texas, while Stacy is from south Louisiana. Faith can fill you in on the rest."

She couldn't help but be impressed with Max's attention to detail, especially without the campers' files as a cheat sheet. Hopefully she could get to know the girls as quickly. Faith already had a huge one up on her. But this wasn't a competition. She and Faith, as perfect as the younger woman seemed, were on the same team.

Still…she watched as Faith led the campers toward the barn. "Is Faith married?"

Max frowned, revealing his confusion as to why it mattered, but didn't question it. "Yes, and she has two small children at home. That's why she's only part-time."

Emma refused to admit why that suddenly made her a lot more open to having Faith as a friend.

After unpacking her suitcase, downing her headache medicine and dozing off for a half hour, Emma felt ready to face the world. Or at least her ex-boyfriend, his perfectly perky counselor and three sullen teen girls.

On second thought, maybe she should have napped longer.

She opened the dorm's front door and was nearly barreled over by Stacy, Tonya and Katie as they hurried inside. She stepped back, offering an easy smile despite the teens' instant suspicion.

"Who are you?" Tonya crossed slim arms over her chest, frowning. "And why are you in our dorm?"

"Silly." Katie hip-bumped Tonya out of the way and grinned at Emma. Her red hair and freckles made her seem younger than Max had indicated, while Tonya's flawless, cocoa-colored skin and braided locks made her appear years older. "She's one of the moms. Remember?" She snapped her fingers. "That cute little guy."

"You're Cody's mom?" Stacy, who had shouldered past on her way toward the bedrooms, stopped and looked back with surprise. "They allowed parents here again? I thought all of y'all left yesterday." Her eyes widened as if worried her own guardian might pop back up unannounced.

Emma sighed. Apparently Max hadn't been able to make the announcement during her nap, or at least not in front of all the campers. All the more reason she should have stuck to tomorrow's plan. Hopefully he'd at least been able to warn Cody.

She forced a smile she didn't feel, ignoring the

fact that she very likely might already be in over her head. "Yes, I'm Cody's mom, but that's irrelevant right now. Max needed a full-time counselor for you girls, so he asked me to step in. I'll be taking over for the woman that went on maternity leave."

"You're the replacement?" Tonya snorted. "Maybe that's why Cody looked so bummed earlier. I'd be, too."

Katie nudged her, mouth open in overly dramatic shock. "Don't be rude!"

"Just being honest." Tonya held up both hands in defense.

Yeah, Emma knew that kind of honesty—and it wasn't steeped in truth. She tightened her smile. "Cody will be fine. Besides, I'm here for you girls. I'm a licensed psychologist."

"Who obviously can't control her own son." Stacy smirked and pushed open the door leading to the bedrooms. "Come on, girls. Dinner's almost ready." She peered over her shoulder as the door began to shut. "Better hurry before Ms. Psychologist tries to shrink our heads."

The click of the door separating her from the teenagers felt like an insurmountable wall, and for a long moment, Emma considered turning and leaving. She swallowed the dismay bubbling in her stomach and worked to keep back the familiar tears of failure. Dinner might be almost ready, but she already felt as if she'd been chewed up and spit out.

But no. This was her chance. The girls were baiting her, testing her. Especially Stacy, who already demonstrated leadership influence on the other girls by being the oldest in the camp. If she let them pull rank now, the next month would be torture on her—and useless for them. They'd all lose.

She shoved aside the personal barb and followed the girls inside, briefly wondering where Faith was and why the girls were even walking around the ranch alone in the first place. Was that against the rules? She'd have to ask Max. So much she didn't know.

But she knew how to handle this.

Her heavy footsteps brought all three girls' heads up. Stacy, where she perched on the edge of her bed changing her shoes; Tonya, where she examined her complexion in the room's only full-length mirror; and Katie, who rummaged through her top dresser drawer.

Emma took advantage of their surprise and squared her shoulders. "Here's how it's going to be." She lifted her chin and crossed her arms, purposefully coming across defensive in her body language. First step, lay down the rules. Set the standard. "I'm in charge here, whether you girls like it or not, and whether you think I deserve to be or not. That's not your decision to make, it's Max's. And it's been made."

She drew a breath, maintaining eye contact with them all, especially Stacy, whom she had the farthest to go to reach. Second step, initiate heart. "We can do this the easy way or the hard way. Personally, I'd like to have fun with you girls. I'm not here to braid hair and paint fingernails and be your best friend. But I really don't want to be a dictator, either."

That seemed to reach Katie, whose expression flickered briefly before morphing back to neutral.

Emma held her breath, intentionally uncrossing her arms, wanting to appear open and approachable. Third step, issue invitation. "What do y'all say to meeting in the middle?"

Silence registered, as all the girls plucked at loose threads in their jeans or on their bed comforters.

So it wasn't going to be that easy. Maybe she needed to play a little dirty. She shifted her weight to one side and tilted her head casually to the other. "I know you're all really loyal to Faith, but can't you give me a chance?"

Katie jerked her head up so fast, her short red hair flew across her cheeks. "What? We barely know Faith."

"But I've seen you with her already, all buddy-buddy." She glanced at Stacy, who frowned slightly. She knew that would get to the older teen. The last thing the rebellious girl wanted would be to seem like she was in tight with an authority figure. Emma shrugged as though it didn't matter. "I guess that's only fair. After all, she seems pretty cool." Max certainly thought so, anyway.

"Faith isn't cool. She's a mom." The words flew out of Stacy's lips so quickly, she was done talking before Emma could even look at her.

She hesitated, not having expected that answer. "I'm a mom."

"Exactly." Stacy leveled her gaze at her. "Moms aren't cool."

"Says who?" She refused to be offended. Though it sort of stung because she knew that was how Cody saw her and that he would only continue seeing her as less and less cool—or admirable, at the least—as he grew up. The thought dug in and twisted.

"Faith isn't that bad." Katie's tentative voice pierced the weighty silence. She played with the dresser drawer pull, letting the metal piece bounce between her fingers and the wood with a steady tap. "She taught you how to stay on your horse today during the trail ride."

"Shut up." The look Stacy shot Katie could have melted concrete. "I didn't need help."

Tonya laughed, finally moving away from the mirror to sit on her bed across from Stacy's. "Yeah, right. You were whiter than those bedsheets."

Stacy threw her shoe at Tonya, who dodged it with a shriek—the first undignified, emotional re- action Emma had seen from the girl yet. Progress in some ways, probably, but she was losing con- trol—if she'd ever had any in the first place. She raised her voice to be heard over the commotion, implementing the next measure in her strategy. "So you guys wouldn't prefer Faith to be your full-time counselor instead of me?"

The looks the girls shot her clearly said they weren't particularly partial to either of them. Perfect. Emma wouldn't be making up ground, but rather, carving her own path. That would make it a lot easier to reach them if she wasn't playing catch-up. "Good."

She should have stopped there, but her mind wouldn't cut the connection to her lips fast enough. Some deep part of her needed these girls to laugh, to like her. To respond to her. To make up for how Cody didn't. She winked. "I promise I won't smile as much as she does, okay?"

Stacy's gaze darted over Emma's shoulder and then dropped to her lap as a reluctant grin spread across her face. She wasn't going to challenge. Score one. Emma glanced at Tonya, who seemed the second-hardest one in the group, and was rewarded with a genuine grin. Or maybe it was another smirk. Oh, well, close enough. Next she looked to Katie, who giggled uncontrollably. Well, that was easy enough.

She'd done it. Won them over for now. Relieved, she allowed herself a moment to relax. "So, how about some dinner?"

"Actually…"

Emma spun around at the sweet voice sounding from behind her. Oh, no.

Faith.

The ponytailed counselor slid her hands on her trim hips and arched one eyebrow at Emma. "I thought we'd just stay in here so I could give smiling lessons."

Chapter Six

Wednesday started early, as evidenced by the chorus of groans as Max paced before his troops, a whistle tucked between his lips. Dew wet the top of his boots, and the late October chill cut through his button-down shirt. He struggled to keep his mind on the yawning teens before him, rather than dwelling on how cute Emma looked first thing in the morning, hair haphazard while wearing jeans and a rumpled sweatshirt. Her charges, though grumpy, were there on the chalked meeting line by the barn, on time and wearing the required work clothes. He was impressed—not bad, since Emma hadn't even gotten the camp schedule until last night at dinner.

Where she'd been quieter than he expected. Maybe her headache hadn't fully gone away by the time they'd been served steaming chicken and dumplings. Then again, did he know anything about Emma well enough anymore to make assumptions? He considered questioning Faith about her, but he didn't want to give the other counselor the wrong idea about him and Emma. He and Emma were definitely no longer "he and Emma."

No matter how much her makeup-free image reminded him of the younger version that still stalked his dreams.

Yeah. Time to get to business.

Max blew the whistle, and Cody clapped his hands over his ears. He fought the wave of sympathy rising in his chest. Growing up, his reaction to sudden sounds had always been the exact same, which got to be embarrassing as he grew older and the mere sound of a chair scraping against the floor in school would be enough to send his hands flying to his head. He eventually broke himself of the habit. Hopefully Cody would, too.

At least the young guy had taken the news of his mom filling in as counselor like a champ. There'd been a hint of panic in Cody's eyes at first, but as Max explained that he would rarely even see Emma besides at mealtimes and during occasional group projects, he'd shrugged it off—probably thinking his easy acceptance would win him brownie points later. Max would have to be careful to keep an eye on that and make sure Cody didn't play Emma against him or vice versa. One hint of that and he'd stop it immediately.

Yesterday, Max was Mr. Nice Guy. Today that would change. He had the teens' best interests at heart—and while their first day had been all about rest time and chicken and dumplings, today, tough love was the main course.

Hopefully Emma would be able to hack it.

He blew the whistle again in two quick successions. "Listen up!" The kids stared blankly, except for Cody, who slowly lowered his hands from his ears and scowled. "First on the agenda is barn chores. Then after breakfast, where you'll receive exactly one half hour to eat, we'll move on to the obstacle course."

That got their attention. Some of the boys grinned and nudged each other with excitement, but the girls looked beyond confused. "Obstacle course?" Katie's red eyebrows nearly disappeared into her matching hairline. "Like, with ropes and barbed wire and stuff?"

"You'll have to wait and see." At one time he'd considered making a separate course for the girls, an easier one, but Nicole had almost taken his head off at the suggestion. Ever since, he'd seen how the girls in each camp had proven themselves time and again. These kids needed a challenge, the girls especially needing to see their own strength, the boys learning how to channel that strength into something positive.

Not for the first time, he wished he'd had someone to drag his teenaged rear end through an obstacle course, to force him to reach beyond himself and for new heights. Then maybe he wouldn't have turned to girls, alcohol and drugs to fill the yawning spaces left behind from his father.

Enough of that. He blew the whistle. "To the barn." The teens groaned, and he silenced them with a look. "All the horses are to be loosed in the paddock. Halters go in the tack room on the hooks. And remember—never approach a horse from the back unless you're partial to getting kicked."

Emma's lips twitched at that one, and he wondered if she was remembering the time he "borrowed" Mr. Judson's mare for a joyride late one night after enjoying too many beers—and gotten exactly what he deserved in the form of a horseshoe imprint on his thigh. His leg twinged at the memory. Yet the most vivid detail of that night was Emma, perched on the fence railing, head tilted and blond hair streaming down her back in the moonlight as she watched for shooting stars.

His gaze darted to her stoic expression in line, and the memory faded. Whatever she'd once seen in him, she certainly didn't anymore. Not that he deserved it—then or now. Sure, he'd turned his life around, but he'd put Emma through the ringer in the meantime. No wonder she deserted him all those years ago. Her temporary draw to the "bad boy next door" had been exactly that—temporary. He never deserved her. Maybe she finally realized that same fact and moved on. Maybe her reasons for never returning had been as simple as that.

With another whistle blow, he herded the kids toward the barn, wishing with all his heart that some mistakes weren't permanent.

Max had failed to mention that as chaperone, Emma was obligated to interact with the teens in the midst of their projects. Riding horses, brushing horses, cleaning stalls—and, apparently, crawling under barbed wire.

She winced as once again her hair snagged in the fencing above her head. She propped on one elbow in the dirt and reached up to free the tangle with her other hand, trying to note where her girls had gone. Katie and Stacy had taken to the course as if they'd already been through military basic training, flawlessly running the tires and scooting under the barbed wire like a couple of prairie dogs.

At least the exertion had fought against the mid-morning chill in the air. She could feel most of her toes, though not many of her fingers. Probably because they were half-buried in the earth. So much for her last manicure.

Though at the moment, nail care was the least of her worries. Some counselor she was, having already lost over half her group. She could only hope they had gone ahead with the rest of the boys who had finished the course. She couldn't raise her head far enough right now to check.

"Need help?"

She tilted her head and peered as far sideways as she could without risking another tangle or mouthful of dirt. Faith, bright-eyed and exhilarated, grinned from her position a yard or two away, looking as if she did this kind of thing every day.

"You probably think I deserve this." Emma wasn't sure which rubbed worse—her verbal blunder in front of the fellow counselor at the dorms yesterday, or the sand currently gritting in her teeth.

Faith army-crawled toward her and laughed. "I know I smile a lot. It's my trademark." She reached over and freed another piece of Emma's hair she hadn't even realized was stuck. "I can't be angry at you for noticing."

"I really wasn't making fun of you." Emma felt about three inches tall, which was pretty accurate seeing how she was crawling through cold mud. "I just—"

"Wanted the girls to like you?" Faith motioned for them to keep going, and Emma pushed herself to follow the younger woman's lead as they neared the end of the course. "I felt the same way when I started here last year. All this pressure to 'fix' these kids at whatever cost." She crawled a few more paces, then slid out from under the last string of wire and stood, offering her hand to Emma. "I forgot that fixing them wasn't in my job description."

Emma accepted the offer, then slid to her feet and started to brush the dirt off her clothes before realizing the effort was futile. If helping the teenagers wasn't the counselors' job, then whose was it? She met Faith's frank, open stare and raised her eyebrows in silent question.

Faith crossed her arms over her stained T-shirt. "I had to remember that was God's job."

Oh.

"I'm here to guide them—but I'm not responsible for their success." She hesitated. "Or their failure."

Great. Now she felt about two inches tall. This was a faith-centered camp, and she'd already tried to usurp God by her own efforts—and made fun of a fellow counselor in the process.

Emma swallowed, ignoring the aftertaste of dirt—and crow. "You're right. That's priority." Or it needed to be, anyway. But how could she lead by an example she wasn't following herself?

Faith started to speak, but a muffled cry sounded from behind them. Emma turned to see Tonya still attempting to make it through the barbed wire course. Despite the teen's lithe figure, she struggled to progress—likely because of having less muscle tone capable of pulling her forward. Emma knew; she had faced the same problem. Sitting in her office, seeing patients the past several years in a row had clearly done nothing for her endurance.

Or apparently, her own emotional health.

Emma shook off the guilt and focused on Tonya. "Use your knees." She immediately dropped to her own, her faded jeans sinking into the dirt, and gestured to Tonya through the rows of barbed wire. "Dig in with your forearms, not just your elbows."

Tonya let out a muffled cry of defeat, her face twisted into a mask of helplessness. Gone was the facade of "I've got it all together," the masked image of "I belong on a runway." Suddenly, she resembled exactly what she was—a scared, dirt-streaked young girl. "I can't."

Well, she had to, unless Max was willing to cut the course apart to get her out. Emma glanced at him across the field, several yards away, blowing his whistle as the group gathered at the next challenge. Somehow, she didn't figure he would.

Faith touched Emma's shoulder and she jerked, having almost forgotten the counselor was there. "Do you need me?"

Emma couldn't express how much she appreciated that trust—so undeserved. She shook her head. "No, I'll talk her out. Don't worry."

"I wasn't worried in the least." Faith proved her statement by wiggling her fingers in a wave and heading toward the rest of the group without a single glance back.

It was up to Emma.

She directed her attention back to Tonya. "You *can* do it. I know you're tired, but it's a lot better on this side. Trust me." There was a metaphor somewhere in that, but neither of them had the time to go there now. Next crisis, maybe.

Tears slipped down the teen's beautiful, cocoa-colored cheeks, and she squeezed her eyes shut. "I'm dizzy."

Probably from stress. A lot of her patients mani-
fested stress physically through headaches, nausea
or dizziness. Emma leaned forward on her knees,
tilting her head to meet Tonya's bleary gaze. "Try
again. Slowly."

Tonya shook her head rapidly. Great. Now her
hair was threatening to tangle, and if that happened,
Emma might as well go grab some wire cutters.
There was only one thing to do. With a resigned
breath, she lowered herself flat on her stomach and
began crawling into the dreaded course to meet her.

Surprise highlighted Tonya's glistening eyes.
"You came back." Relief saturated her voice so
completely Emma couldn't help but smile.

"I'm on your team." She held the teen's gaze to
make her point, then tapped her dirt-caked hands.
"Now dig."

Tonya's lips pursed and she took a deep breath,
then began pulling herself forward.

"Forearms."

She adjusted her form and Emma began to crawl
backward to get out of her way. After several
bogged moments in the mud, they finally slipped
under the end of the wires together and stood.

"Thanks." A red flush tinted Tonya's face and
she looked down, then away, the mask vacant but
starting to flicker. "You know, for doing that. Coming back in and everything."

The immediate expression of gratitude still
caught Emma off guard. She wanted to turn the

incident into a lesson, but sometimes, the best lessons learned were the ones that weren't forced. "No woman gets left behind."

A surprised smile quirked the corners of Tonya's mouth, then faded. "Not everyone thinks so." Her gaze darted to her teammates, who Emma could now clearly see were well on their way to the next event.

"You'll realize, probably sooner than you want, that friends don't always make the best choices." She flicked her hand to dismiss her before Tonya could revert to distant default. Emma wanted to leave this battlefield one step ahead. "Go on, now. The next challenge awaits."

"I'm pretty sure a significant one was already met."

She spun around at Max's voice in such close proximity. "Max." Her heart raced, and she squeezed her cold fingers into a fist. He still had the ability to get her blood pressure up.

She refused to ponder why.

His eyes warmed as they drew her in. Vaguely, she noticed Tonya jogging toward her group, but really, all she could take in was the way Max's T-shirt hugged his muscles. He'd apparently shed the work shirt from earlier that morning, and the heather-gray color did dangerous things to his eyes.

And her heart.

He smiled, oblivious to the reaction she fought so hard in his presence. Anger, that was it. It had to be a weird visceral response to the years of bitterness toward him. Nothing more. Not attraction. Not curiosity.

Definitely not regret.

He ran his hand briefly over his hair, cowboy-hat free in honor of the course. "That was great." He gestured toward the barbed wire course with a tanned arm. "Faith told me Tonya was having trouble but that you had it under control."

Yet he still had to come see for himself? Well, she couldn't hold that against him. Other things, yes, but not that.

She forced a smile in return. "She just needed some encouragement."

"I saw you go get her." Max reached out and briefly touched her arm. The graze of his fingers burned and she jerked automatically away from the impact. "A lot of ground was covered. And not just literally. I'm impressed."

"I did what anyone would do." She crossed her arms to avoid another congratulating pat, not sure she had enough bitterness riled up at the moment to be a sufficient barrier. Her heart soared at the thought she'd actually made a difference toward Tonya, and that she'd made the right choice in how she'd handled the girl's struggle. Maybe she could do some good at the camp after all.

Yet that good mood lowered her defenses, and with a secret the size of hers, she had to stay on guard.

Max shook his head. "I think most counselors would have talked her through it from the sidelines. You dove back into the game."

She'd never been one for sports analogies, but she got his point. "I'm glad you're not regretting hiring me." Wait a minute, she wasn't getting paid. She fumbled for the right words. "Or not hiring me. I mean, asking me to volunteer." Perfect. Maybe if she kept talking, she could actually fit her foot in her mouth.

A slow grin lit Max's face, and her stomach reluctantly flipped. "I don't regret *that* at all."

His emphasis on the word made her breath hitch, and she rolled in her bottom lip. The weight of her secret suddenly resembled a thousand anvils taking residence on her shoulders—too heavy to bear. Had she been wrong? About everything?

No. She blinked, reminding herself of the memories she dredged up regularly to starve the guilt. Drugs. Guns. Bad guys. She'd saved her son.

But exactly how far was Cody from that now, anyway?

Max's expression suddenly shadowed. "Uh-oh. Looks like Cody's having trouble on the rope swing."

She followed his gaze to the challenge ahead, where the rest of the teams had gathered with Chaplain Tim, Faith and another male counselor whose name escaped her. The joy she'd known from helping Tonya bled from her heart like water through a sieve. She could hear the taunting of Cody's fail-ure on the rope from some of the other boys, and compassion mixed with her natural mama-bear in-stincts. *No one* made fun of her son. She rushed forward.

"I've got it."

His protest didn't deter her and she pressed on. "I have to—"

Max's brow furrowed and he grasped her wrist to stop her. "I said, I've got it." The warning in his eyes spoke volumes, reminding her of her place. She might have made a significant step with Tonya, but the proof was in the pudding—or more accu-rately, the bog. And right now her son was dangling above it, trapped and scorned.

Proving once again that she could help everyone in the world except for those she loved the most.

Chapter Seven

It was the same in every camp—it never took long for the group to find the weakest link and stage an attack. Now the guys who had taunted Cody were raking the front yard as punishment, while the rest of the campers were allowed an hour of free time before dinner—their only break after an entire day of barn chores, the obstacle course, hiking and the individual chats with him he dubbed One4One.

Max folded his arms and leveled his gaze at Cody, who could have been enjoying some video games or watching a movie had he not gotten in trouble, but was instead washing Max's work truck. A trace of guilt still lingered over the way he'd stopped Emma so abruptly that morning, but she couldn't go barreling over to save the day for her son. Talk about making matters worse for a guy. Plus, it was Max's issue to handle. Emma had proven herself in the incident with Tonya, but even with the girls, she wouldn't have final say in everything that came up. Volunteers were volunteers. Necessary, yes, but the bottom line came down to the kids, God—and Max.

He had a lot of making up to do there.

Speaking of making up—he hoped Emma wouldn't be mad at him. He had only done what he had to in order to stop her from making a mistake, but that look in her eyes still taunted his soul. It'd been one part confusion, two parts hurt, all topped with a healthy heaping of doubt. Emotions he could recognize a mile away.

He should know, he saw them in the mirror often enough.

"This stinks." Cody let out another, stronger word as he sloshed a bucket of water against the driver's side door and halfheartedly rubbed it with a sponge. The water hose tangled on the gravel drive at his feet. Max considered suggesting that he un-kink it before turning the water back on but held the advice inside. The kid would figure it out when it wouldn't flow.

And just like the hose, he needed to figure out what was clogging Cody.

"You do understand why you're out here, don't you?" He tugged the brim of his hat lower over his eyes to block the glare of the afternoon sun reflecting off the windshield.

Cody shrugged, water dripping down his forearms and leaving dirty trails. He glared. "Because I said those bad words on the rope swing?"

"Hardly." Max snorted. "You just said a bad word ten seconds ago and didn't even notice."

Cody remained silent, scrubbing at a mud streak on the truck door with more attention than it really required. Was he listening, finally? Max shifted his weight, wishing he'd brought a chair outside to pull up and level with the kid. But there'd be time enough for that during their One4One tomorrow. "You'd have been punished for the cursing, too, but not as severely. You're out here because when you got off the rope, you swung at Peter."

"And missed." Cody shot him a pointed glance, as if his bad aim should excuse him.

"Sometimes, intention matters more than result." A fact he wished he could go back and alter in his own life. If only these kids could glimpse five years, ten years into the future—man, what changes they'd make. "Trying to hit him is as bad as doing it."

The sponge splashed into the bucket, spraying water on Max's boots as Cody straightened to his full height. "It's not fair! He was laughing at me. They all were."

Not all, but Max could imagine it felt that way, hanging above a crowd and demonstrating to everyone that he couldn't hack the challenge. Cody was the youngest, and smallest, kid in the camp. Physically, he was behind the other guys, but in spirit, he could rise far above—if only he'd properly channel that frustration and rage. Max had been the same way when he was in junior high, having not grown into his tall frame until later in his teen years. It stung being the smallest kid on the team in a culture obsessed with equating muscles with masculinity.

But if he'd been told there were more important things to consider at the age of thirteen, would he have listened any better than Cody? If his dad had told him…maybe. Too late to ever know now. And from the blank line on Cody's paperwork regarding his father, well, the kid wouldn't get to discover that theory for himself, either.

Once again, he and Cody were in the same holey boat.

But Max hadn't sunk to the bottom, and he was determined that Cody—and the rest of the kids in his charge this month—wouldn't, either. He drew a steadying breath, praying for patience and wisdom. "How'd you feel, when they laughed at you?"

Cody picked up the hose, fumbling with the nozzle and averting his eyes. "I didn't care."

"No lying at Camp Hope."

He let out a huff. "Fine. I felt stupid. Happy now?"

"Not really." Max waited a beat, understanding the frustration that drove the teen's illogical outbursts. They'd work on that together. But first things first. "Why did you feel stupid?"

"Because I couldn't do it. And everyone else could."

Definitely wasn't the time to point out the girls

had struggled with the challenge, except Stacy, who'd shown surprising strength and made it across the bog on her first try. "It's not about what everyone else does. It's about *your* effort. And if you hadn't come down off the rope trying to land punches, I'd have been proud of how hard you tried."

Cody's hands stilled on the water hose. "Really?" The gruff tone attempted to camouflage the hope under the words but failed.

Max pretended not to notice. "Yeah, man. And besides, not being able to do something challenging on the first try doesn't make you stupid. But handling it the way you did makes you a quitter."

"Let me guess." Cody tried to spray the truck, but the water clogged as Max had predicted. He looked at the length of hose and finally knelt to untwist it. "No quitting at Camp Hope, either."

Max grinned. "You're a fast learner. And that's why you're going to try again tomorrow."

Panic flashed across Cody's face before he unleashed the water on the truck. The spray created a mist against the sunlight. "Do I have to?"

"You want to be a quitter? Feel stupid?"

He shook his head, staring down at the river of soapy suds sliding across the gravel.

"Remember—everyone does things at their own pace, in their own time. You're here for you." Max reached out and clapped his hand on Cody's shoulder, slightly surprised at the connection he felt toward the little guy. Probably because he was one of the youngest campers he'd ever had at the ranch—and maybe because so much of Cody reminded him of himself as a teenager. If he could keep these guys from making some of his mistakes, it'd all be worth it.

"Just keep trying." He patted Cody's shoulder before dropping his hand to his side. "And keep your fists to yourself."

Cody smirked but didn't argue as he shut off the water. "If you say so."

"There's just one more thing." Max plastered on his most serious expression, effective enough that Cody's face fell.

"What is it?" He squinted as if bracing himself.

Max gestured to the truck, holding back a grin. "You missed a spot."

He totally deserved the wet sponge that splattered against his stomach.

Despite the day of heavy physical activity, Emma couldn't sleep. She adjusted the pillow under her head for the tenth time, wondering if Katie were going to snore every night or if this was an exception. Across the room from her bunk, Stacy muttered in her sleep, her deep Southern accent giving an odd rhythm to the half-formed words, while Tonya lay quietly, a pink glittered sleep mask covering her eyes.

Emma rolled over, pulled the blanket over her

ears, and squeezed her eyes shut. But all she could see in her mind's eye was a replay of Cody swinging helplessly from a rope, the expression on his face a mixture of anger, embarrassment and fear.

She sat up abruptly before she could picture the same expression paired with an orange jumpsuit, and swung her legs over the side of the bed. Maybe some water or milk from the kitchen would settle her nerves and help her sleep. A distraction was necessary, regardless. She couldn't keep lying in bed alternating between regretting the past and wishing away the future.

Including the regret of not having slammed past Max when he'd stopped her from getting involved with Cody.

Max asked her to come to the camp as a favor— for him, of all people—then expected her to look the other way when her child was hurting and in need? When Cody was made out to be a target? When the last thing he needed at the camp was more reason to grow angry and bitter and distant?

Though deep down, she couldn't ignore the sensation that Max had a point. Underneath the surface layers of mama-bear instincts and desperation lay the truth—she'd have made things worse.

Still, that didn't take away the incessant desire to fix it. Fix Cody.

Fix herself.

Maybe she'd make that milk a hot chocolate.

Emma threw on a flannel robe, knotted it at her

waist and shoved her feet into the closest shoes she could find—her shower flip-flops. The night air would be chilly, but she'd rush to the kitchen and be back before she had time to get cold—or before the girls could wake up and realize she'd left.

She hesitated at the door, one hand grazing the knob, and studied her sleeping charges. Still snoring. Still unmoving. Nothing to worry about—after all, hadn't Faith left the girls alone for a short time yesterday, before barging in and catching Emma in her verbal blunder? They'd be fine.

Careful not to let the door slam, Emma slipped outside the dorm and into the main house. Since Mama Jeanie did all the cooking and served their meals, Emma hadn't had reason to rummage through the refrigerator yet and didn't know where anything was in the kitchen. Probably wouldn't find it in the pitch black. She flipped on the low light over the sink, brightening the stone tiles on the floor. The room felt different this late at night, and she tiptoed quietly toward the refrigerator, aware that Mama Jeanie's sleeping quarters weren't far down the hall.

She quickly found the milk, searched in vain for a bottle of chocolate syrup and finally discovered a drinking glass in the cabinet to the right of the pantry. She took a big gulp of plain milk just as heavy footsteps sounded on the stairs.

Pausing midsip, she stared at Max over the rim of her glass.

He raised his eyebrows, the corner of his mouth quirked as amusement danced in his eyes. His wrinkled T-shirt and pajama pants, along with rumpled hair void of its usual cowboy hat, gave testament to his own lack of sleep. "Thirsty?"

A flush heated her neck, and she swiped her mouth with the sleeve of her robe. Juvenile, but faster than trying to find a paper napkin—and better than conversing with a liquid mustache. "Couldn't sleep."

"Long first day, huh?" He reached for the fridge and pulled out the carton of orange juice.

"You could say that." She stepped back as he rummaged for a cup. Memories long buried burned for release. He'd always preferred juice over milk, regardless of the time of day or food he was eating. Some things never changed.

"I feel like I need to apologize for earlier." Max set the carton back in the fridge and turned to her, sincerity shining in his gaze. He ran his finger around the edge of his full glass, meeting her eyes briefly before averting them.

She threw him a proverbial bone, however grudgingly. "You did the right thing." The words tasted unfamiliar. Max Ringgold, making the right decision? But she had to somehow let go of the Max she knew from the past and reconcile it with the one standing before her now. Old Max drank orange juice out of the carton, cared about nothing but his own next adventure—illegal or not—and lived for the moment.

New Max poured juice into cups, helped troubled teens and ran a successful ministry.

Somewhere in between the two extremes lay a missing puzzle piece, and Emma couldn't help but long to find out where it went. Where it fit.

What hole it might fill.

He picked up his glass but still didn't drink, rather studied it as if the yellow liquid held answers. "I wasn't apologizing for the why, but the what. I was abrupt."

Well that sounded more like the Max she knew. But this one wasn't arrogant, only confident. There was a difference if one looked hard enough.

She just didn't think it wise to stick around and try.

"It was the right choice." She took another quick sip of milk and rinsed her glass in the sink. "No worries." There was so much more she wanted to say, but standing in a dark kitchen with Max in their pajamas didn't exactly lend to the right timing.

"I know it's awkward."

She hesitated, her back to him as she turned off the faucet. She didn't want to turn around, didn't want to risk seeing something in his eyes she only once imagined she'd see—change. Pure, heartfelt, hard-core change. Max had clearly made something of himself, had chosen a better path after she abandoned their sinking ship of a relationship by escaping to college and never looking back. She'd wanted to see that change in him so bad then but had gotten burned. He'd not only broken his promise to her to change, he'd flat-out mocked it. How could he whisper such heartfelt assurances of her being good for him, of her being enough—and then turn around and do another drug deal the minute he thought her back was turned?

It was too late.

And she couldn't bear seeing the change in person when it couldn't undo the past.

She lowered her eyes as she turned, wiping her hands on the sides of her robe. "What's awkward?" Denial at its worst. But what choice did she have? None of the events of the past few days made any sense to her heart, already fragile and weary from the strain of Cody's rebellion.

"Us."

She lifted her gaze, grateful for the shadows shrouding his half of the kitchen, and moved away from the light lest he see too much. "It's just a month." That currently felt as if it'd already been about six. Sort of reminded her of another time in her life where nine months went by as slowly as a decade. Her cheeks burned.

"There was just so much…left…" Max coughed and took a long drink from his glass. He didn't bother to finish his sentence when he set it back on the counter.

"Between us." The words drifted from her

mouth, as lazy as a warm wind on a summer's day. She didn't even mean to say them. But they hung in the gap.

"You left." His voice barely rose above the hum of the ice machine kicking on in the freezer. "And you never came back."

A fist of tension closed around her throat, and she opened her mouth, unsure what to say or what she even could say at this point without ruining everything. Blinking rapidly, she stared at him, anxiety pressing in on her chest.

He moved toward her, as if taking her silence for regret. And was there regret? Plenty. But not in the way he'd anticipate.

She held up one hand as he drew nearer, her fingers grazing the muscles of his chest beneath his T-shirt. "That's not true." If he came closer, she'd forget who she was, where she was—how *old* she was—and slam right back into the past. Straight back into the body of her naive, eighteen-year-old self who couldn't see that her daddy was right about more than she wanted to admit. Who couldn't see that flirting with fire guaranteed burns.

Who couldn't look past the chemistry with Max still currently flushing her cheeks.

Even back then there'd been this innate urge to fix people. To see past the surface and reach through the exterior to the heart of someone hurting. As a young adult, Max had hurt. And she'd been drawn to him, convinced she'd turn him around. It brought a sense of purpose, knowing she'd made a difference in someone's life when she couldn't do a thing to help her own family's problems. She couldn't pad the checking account or convince the stubborn soil to yield produce for her father—but maybe she could heal with love.

She just never thought she'd get sucked in. That the darkness would overcome the light, that the single step she took down a path would pull her along until she was miles deep.

"You came back?" He took a step away from her, whether out of shock or because of her raised hand she couldn't tell. "When?"

She couldn't answer that one. Not now. What could she say? *I came back to tell you I was pregnant with Cody and caught you in the middle of a drug deal with one of the area's "most wanted"?* She hesitated, and he filled in his own blank.

"For your dad's funeral."

That was true. She'd been there and stayed as incognito as possible.

She didn't even get a chance to nod before he wrapped her in a hug. "I'm sorry I didn't know you were here." His strong arms curled around her waist and held her tight. "I'd have come and found you."

The heartfelt words sank into her dry heart like a desert rain and soaked in deep. She returned the hug automatically, hands pressed against the hard contours of his back, certain he felt her heart pounding out of control under her robe. He radiated warmth, familiarity, memories…

No. *No*. She was back in Max Ringgold's arms, after-hours. Maybe some things had changed, but apparently not enough.

She jerked away. "I've got to check on the girls." She flew through the kitchen door, wincing as the screen slammed behind her.

The perfect punctuation to the turmoil in her heart.

Chapter Eight

If Max batted zero one more time with Emma Shaver, he'd make some kind of unfortunate, proverbial hall of fame. She'd pulled out of his arms faster than he'd run out of church the first time Brady dragged him—and with just as many fears etched across her face.

But not before she hugged him back. Not before she'd fit against him like a missing puzzle piece from his past. As if the past decade plus hadn't separated them at all.

And that might be the scariest part.

He adjusted his cowboy hat as he leaned against the door frame of the recreation room, where he supervised the kids' free time. He really needed to get his mind off Emma and what transpired—or almost transpired—in the kitchen last night and back on the kids before him. All but two were enjoying the rewards of their hard work and the bonus system he'd put into place last year. For each good deed done or extra mile taken in conduct toward their peers, they were awarded an extra ten minutes of free time for the week.

The two that hadn't earned any rewards yet, Peter and Ashton, were in the kitchen helping Mama Jeanie—peeling potatoes for soup that night. Mama Jeanie always made soup on Fridays. She said in life, it was the little things you could count on that meant the most. And that these kids coming through the program needed stability, needed to be able to depend on the little things, so she made soup.

There was probably a lot of genius in that.

Max shifted his weight, watching as David and Hank shot a puck at rapid speed across the air hockey table. Luke always loved playing that game with the teens. Thankfully Nicole's doctor had put her on bed rest at the hospital, so Luke still had a little bit of freedom to help out at the ranch periodically while she rested. He'd be there tomorrow for the next group trail ride and could fill in with the boys while Max did more One4One sessions. He couldn't wait to meet with Cody again so they could dig deeper on the issues the boy had. He'd barely scratched the surface, but Max could tell that the lack of a father figure in Cody's life had affected him. How badly, he had yet to determine.

Sometimes he wasn't sure if physically absent fathers were better or worse than the emotionally absent ones like his own had been.

His eyes drifted toward the younger boy, who lounged on the couch in front of the TV, fingers furiously punching at the Xbox controls. Cody's speed and concentration were testament that the fast-paced car game on the screen wasn't his first rodeo. The kid definitely had a mind geared toward technology—though in the past few days, Max had noticed his confidence increase with the animals, as well. He had the capability to be well-rounded, but clearly the video games and iPod buds were a bigger draw. Hopefully they'd break through that before the end of the camp, since the violence utilized in most of those games—and the lyrics of the music Cody chose—didn't lend to good behavior. In fact, he was surprised Emma hadn't made more rules about those choices.

And then she was there, as if his thinking about her had drawn her. Her fresh, peppermint scent wafted past him as she peered around the door frame into the room, her blond hair sweeping her shoulders. "Are the girls okay?"

Emma's tone, all business, doused the spark of hope that had birthed last night. He eased aside to give her space, though his instincts warred inside him to press closer. But it was like working with a frightened filly—pushing only led to someone getting trampled.

He forced what he hoped looked like a casual smile and hoped she couldn't tell that just minutes ago he'd been psychoanalyzing her child. "The girls have been playing board games. Tonya seemed to get bored and hit the treadmill earlier, but now I think the competition is pretty fierce." He gestured toward where the girls were gathered in one corner of the room, hunched over a board with multiple pieces. Katie frowned as she rolled the game dice, while Stacy grinned as she counted her wad of paper money.

Emma acknowledged the update with a slight nod, though she still didn't meet his eyes. Probably a good thing, too. At this proximity, with last night still fresh in his mind, he might forget his batting average altogether and do something crazy—like kiss her. Just to see if the sparks they'd once lit like the Fourth of July were still flammable. To see if he could detect even a hint of their old relationship like he'd imagined he'd felt in her hug.

To see if there was any reason at all to reignite the embers he'd never been able to fully put out.

He kept his eyes on the room of kids, the knot in his throat growing until he thought he'd choke. The tense silence between them spoke more than most words could, and he hated what the message relayed. "You ready for the trail ride tomorrow?" Not the most genius of topics, but at least it broke the ice freezing him out.

She stiffened beside him at the reminder of the horses. "Ready as I'll ever be to sit on top of a moving beast."

"Come on, now. You've ridden before." Settled

in front of him while they rode bareback together, if he remembered correctly. And he didn't forget most things involving Emma Shaver.

She met his eyes then, with a pointed look that shot like a barb into his heart. "And it's *still* not my cup of tea."

Ouch. Point taken.

Definitely not the time to remind her she'd once ridden on his friend's Harley, either.

He opened his mouth to say something, anything to get her head away from the negative past, when one of the biggest boys in the camp, sixteen-year-old Jarvis Mason, sat down suddenly on the couch next to Cody. "My turn."

Cody wrangled the controller slightly out of reach, his eyes never leaving the TV screen as the race car continued careening at high speeds around a digital track. "Not yet."

"Come on, you've been playing ever since we got in here." Jarvis reached for the controller, crowding his space as Cody jerked it away once again.

Uh-oh. Max felt Emma's eyes bore into the side of his face, gauging, judging, waiting for him to intervene. But he wouldn't, not yet. In the real world, he wouldn't be there to run interference for these kids. They had to learn to handle opposition and conflict in a healthy way, and after the talk he'd had with Cody the other day by his truck, he was confident Cody could make the right decision.

He crossed his arms and waited, believing. *Come on, Cody. Make good choices.*

Jarvis sneered and used muscle this time, elbowing Cody in the side and snatching the controller for himself. "Time for little boys to share."

Cody lunged, like a bull from a chute, straight at Jarvis's barrel chest. Jarvis yelled in surprise, and, with his hands full of the game controller, couldn't dodge the scrawny fist Cody shot right at his nose.

Apparently Max had been wrong.

Emma sucked in her breath, hands covering her mouth. Blood dripped from Jarvis's nose, and with a growl, he threw down the controller. The room stilled, and Katie gasped. Several of the other guys stood up, whether to jump in to help or make it worse, Max wasn't certain. To Cody's credit, he only lifted his chin and met Jarvis's gaze head-on as they glared at each other in front of the TV.

This would be the time to intervene.

Max covered the distance between him and the boys in three long strides. "That's enough, guys. Game over." He took the controller and tossed it out of reach on the floor.

"He *punched* me." Jarvis wiped his face, red streaking across his cheek, and his eyes narrowed to slits.

Cody scoffed. "Because you deserved it."

"I saw what happened." Max raised his voice over the sound of Jarvis's high-pitched protests. "Stacy, could you throw me those tissues, please?"

She tossed the box at him from across the room. Max caught it deftly in one hand and plucked several for Jarvis, who pressed the thin tissues against his face.

Max could almost feel the trembles racking Cody's body, whether from adrenaline or shame he couldn't be sure. But these boys needed separation, quick.

He hooked his arm through Cody's elbow and tugged the boy to one side, halfway behind him. Jarvis could still retaliate, and from the looks in both boys' eyes, he wouldn't be surprised if they acted first and gladly accepted punishment later. He couldn't risk any more blood.

He nodded at Emma, who stepped uncertainly into the room, eyes glued to Cody as if she weren't sure if she could go to him or not.

She couldn't.

Max coughed intentionally, drawing her gaze. "Please take Jarvis to Chaplain Tim in the dorms." Away from here. Away from Cody, before the older teen realized he'd just been bested by a thirteen-year-old and tried to outmuscle them all. The last thing Max needed was a dog pile, and some of the other boys in the room still pressed in closer than he liked, the excitement of a fight lighting their eyes.

Emma's lips pursed into a line, but just like he knew she would, she snapped out of mama-mode and into counselor-mode. "Sure." Her tone grew firm and impossible to argue with. "Come on,

Jarvis." She held out a steady hand, ushering him toward the door.

"I get punched in the face, and *I* have to see the preacher man?" The bigger boy's voice rose to a crescendo, but he didn't argue further as he tossed crimson tissues in the trash can they walked past. "Totally unfair."

"We'll talk soon. Don't worry." Max waited until they left the room, keeping one hand on Cody's shoulder, and met the gaze of the other boys in the room. "Back to your games. Or you can all peel potatoes."

The group instantly broke up and went back to their activities. Max couldn't leave with Cody, though, not until Emma got back or Faith or the other part-timers came on duty. With this much tension in the air, no way was he leaving any of the teens unsupervised. He'd seen it plenty of times—one broke a rule, and the others were tempted to follow close behind. It was that carnal temptation to push the limits. Sort of like how Max had been the majority of his life until the Lord wrangled it out of him.

Even now, though, wasn't he doing the same thing with Emma? Wanting to push, test his limits, see how close he could get to winning her back?

No. He couldn't go there right now.

He led Cody to a corner of the room that wasn't occupied and turned his full attention to the boy. The pained glaze in his eyes felt hauntingly familiar. Max had been the same way growing up—it was like looking in a mirror from years ago, all that hurt and sadness bottled behind a thick wall of defense. If it hadn't been for Brady and his influence—not to mention Emma's—Max would still be in big trouble. Who would be "Brady" to Cody? Who would knock down those walls?

He wanted to do it. But one month in a camp wasn't always long enough. Yet somehow, Max felt more compelled to try than ever before. He sat Cody down on the edge of a chair near the front of the room and took the ottoman across from him, pulling it up so their knees nearly touched and their words wouldn't carry. "What gives, man?"

Cody shrugged, an odd mixture of pride and repentance engraved in his expression. "Jarvis is a bully."

Max leaned back slightly, crossing his arms over his chest. "You hit him, though. What does that make you?"

"Smarter?"

He almost laughed, a gut reaction, but he held it at bay. Despite the surprise of the answer, this was serious. Moments like these had eternal consequence. If Cody didn't realize the severity of his choices, he might never turn back. The weight of that wiped any trace of a smile from Max's face. "Wrong answer."

Cody sighed and looked down at his hands. "It's not that big a deal."

"It's sort of a huge deal, Cody." Max waited until the boy looked up, and held his gaze. "That's twice you've either attempted or succeeded at starting a physical fight here at Camp Hope. You know that's against the rules."

Once more and it'd be his third strike. Unless Max and the other counselors met and decided to wipe the first offense off his camp record since he didn't actually make contact with Peter at the rope swing. But that could go either way and, regardless, the situation brought Cody way too close to being terminated from the camp. Max had to keep the camp safe for the other campers.

No playing favorites, even if he did feel inexplicably drawn to Cody.

"Am I being kicked out?"

Max couldn't tell if that was his goal or not, and the thought that it could be made him want to simultaneously slap the teen upside his head and hug his neck. He knew where the rebellion was birthed; he'd experienced it himself.

But that didn't make the blatant disrespect and apathy any easier to swallow—especially by those who went out of their way to help hurting kids. Kids who lashed out and hurt others because of their own wounds, like an angry lion with its paw in a trap. Assaulting the one trying to set it free.

Well, Max had his share of battle wounds and wasn't afraid of a few more. Not when it could mean the difference between life and death. "If you want out, you're free to leave." The words were a gamble, but he knew when a scared teenager was bluffing. Cody's sudden wide eyes proved his instincts true. "Hit the road, Jack. Have fun in juvie. I know for a fact the food isn't nearly as good."

Cody's eyes narrowed in defense. "I'm not going to juvie."

"You will if you leave here. This is Last Chance City, and you know it."

The fight momentarily left his eyes, and suddenly the abandoned, lost little boy was all Max could see. He leaned forward, bracing his elbows on his knees, not wanting to lose the momentary breakdown of a wall. "I want you here, Cody. But you have to follow the rules for the program to work. I can't help you if I'm constantly breaking up fights."

Cody traced an aimless pattern on the knee of his jeans with one finger, not responding.

"I need you to meet me halfway." Max held his breath. "And I need you to realize that hitting someone bigger than you doesn't make you better than them. In fact, it makes you pretty small."

The teen's gaze lifted then, doused in hope and confusion. The sight of it nearly broke Max's heart. Had no one ever told him that in a way that he could relate to? But who would have if the boy didn't have a father or even, as far as he knew, a family member or friend taking on the role?

He swallowed the unusual level of empathy he

felt toward Cody and pressed forward with his advice. "Anyone can throw punches and maybe land a few. But it takes a bigger man to walk away and to learn which battles to take on." He paused. "Make sense?"

"Sort of."

"It will. If you just follow my lead and quit attacking people." Max rushed on as Cody's mouth opened in protest. "Even those who you feel attack you first. Trust me, it's the only way."

His shoulders deflated. "Yes, sir."

"And, Cody?"

The boy raised his eyebrows indifferently, but life flickered in his eyes. He cared—whether he wanted to or not.

Max continued before he could get too excited about the fact. "Man to man, I'm here for you. About anything. All right?"

A tiny smile lifted one corner of Cody's mouth before he shoved it aside with his typical, bored expression. He nodded, feigning disinterest.

It still counted. A small victory, but he'd take it. Max stood, relief coursing through his veins, and gestured for Cody to join him. "You know you have a punishment to fulfill now, huh?"

"I figured." Cody sighed and trudged toward the game room door. "Potatoes?"

"Nope. Rope swing." They'd kill two birds with one stone, however pathetically small it might be.

And they'd stay out there until Cody got it right. "Potatoes will be dessert."

He shot the boy a look that silenced his protesting groan and nodded in satisfaction at the "yes, sir" that abruptly followed. One step at a time, whether it was two forward and three back or not.

One thing remained certain—Cody Shaver was going to know what it was like to have a father figure.

Even if only for a month.

She shouldn't have listened. Eavesdropping was wrong, and disrespectful. But after Pastor Tim had intercepted Jarvis in the hallway and she'd gone back to check on Cody, she couldn't help but overhear the words Max murmured urgently to her son. Things she'd been trying to say to him for months but they had fallen on completely disinterested ears. Would Cody listen to Max any better than he had to her? Would it change anything? Detour him from the path he'd started walking down?

He'd attacked Jarvis. The memory made her hands shake. Clearly he'd been provoked, but still— her little boy had jumped another kid. At a camp for troubled teens, no less.

Was this hopeless after all?

She'd nearly gotten caught when they'd abruptly ended their conversation and headed her way. She'd ducked around the corner into the upstairs bathroom, which was thankfully empty, and hid behind the half-closed door until they passed, breathing the smell of the citrus plug-in and trying to calm her erratic heartbeat as Max's words replayed in her head. *I need you to meet me halfway. It takes a bigger man to learn which battles to take on.*

Man to man, I'm here for you.

Her heart constricted until she couldn't breathe. Max had no idea the depth of what he was saying. Not the slightest clue—and it was her fault. But if Cody was starting to respond to him, even slightly, how much more harm would it do to tell the truth now? It wouldn't be letting a cat out of a bag—no, this would be more akin to unleashing a snarling tiger.

On her son.

No. She couldn't do it. No matter how much it hurt to hear Max be tender and compassionate with her son—*his* son—she wouldn't wield a giant red stop sign in front of Cody. Not while there was even a smidgen of hope that this program could save him.

She sagged against the bathroom wall, the towel bar digging into her back. But oh, Max had sounded so…sweet. Strong. Achingly familiar. Like all those nights he'd held her and promised he wanted a life with her. That she was a good influence on him. That he'd change.

Well, he had, sometime over the past thirteen years. And he'd never bothered to let her know.

She stiffened, the scent of the orange air freshener and the adrenaline churning in her stomach strengthening her resolve. This situation wasn't *all* her fault. The door swung both ways, after all, and the other side had never been knocked on. Max could have sought her out if he'd missed her as terribly as he indicated last night in the kitchen. She might have purposefully gone off the grid while pregnant, but there were always ways around that if someone wanted to make the effort badly enough. He could have found her.

The fact that he didn't pursue her after turning his life around said plenty about what she'd actually meant to him. She'd been a good time, just like all the other girls he'd been rumored to be with, and nothing more.

And she knew that going into it. She'd sought Max initially out of rebellion and a skewed sense of need and didn't deserve anything more than the heartache she got. That's what happened when good girls went rogue. God had taught her a lesson, and she'd learned it the hard way—in fact, she was still paying for her mistake.

But she refused to let Cody be a casualty of her spiritual battle. She'd do whatever—*whatever*—it took to make sure he didn't follow in his father's early footsteps. Max would be a good dad to Cody, when the time was right. But that time was not today—even if the memory of their gentle conversation would linger in her ears long after the lights were shut off in the dorm.

She pushed away from the wall. Enough of this mental back-and-forth. She couldn't hide in a bathroom forever, and debating with herself wouldn't accomplish anything. It was time to get back to work. Just because she had to be hands-off with Cody right now didn't mean she couldn't try to help Katie, Tonya and Stacy to the best of her ability. Those girls needed her.

And she needed to be needed.

Emma cautiously peered around the frame before slipping into the hallway. Surely it was safe to come out now.

Though anywhere near Max Ringgold could never be considered safe.

Chapter Nine

The weekend flew by, and with the activities Max had lined up, Emma didn't see him or Cody much.

Thankfully.

Instead, she focused on her girls, and Faith came by for the entire day Saturday to help out with the group projects. Max lightened the intensity of the workload on weekends, meaning the teens—and by default, Emma—got to sleep until eight o'clock in the morning instead of six-thirty. So she and Faith took the girls on a hike, since exercise was required every day, and then messed around at the rock climbing station until all their arms were too achy to continue.

Being outside under the impossibly blue sky had been therapeutic, providing Emma a temporary reprieve from the thoughts that circled as relentlessly as vultures. Her first week at Camp Hope hadn't been boring, that was for sure, though at least Cody hadn't had any more issues—that Max had made her aware of. Who knew what went on in their private counseling sessions? But being with the girls, facing physical challenges and inhaling the wheat-scented country air, made Emma forget the turmoil of seeing Max and Cody together. Forget her son was one breath away from serious trouble.

Forget that the man in the cowboy hat still carried a piece of her heart somewhere in the pocket of his Wranglers.

Now, Monday morning, they were taking their shift in the barn, an hour before the boys would arrive to do their chores. Faith had gone home to her family Saturday night late, meaning she'd missed the optional Sunday morning devotionals. Max didn't force that time on the teens, though he offered rewards for attending, so more than half the group showed up. Stacy and Tonya hadn't wanted to attend, preferring to sleep an extra thirty minutes instead, so Emma stayed with them in the dorm, grateful for the excuse. She didn't know if she was ready to see Max hold a Bible with the same hands he once used to take drugs and hot-wire cars. Her world had been rocked enough the past week. One mind-blowing event at a time.

She paced the barn aisle in a slow rhythm, feeling way too much like a prison warden as she checked the girls' progress on mucking stalls. Stacy, her curly hair pulled back into a messy ponytail, worked hard, though not exactly cheerfully. Tonya hoisted her pitchfork with much slower movements, a sheen of sweat dotting her brow despite the early November chill penetrating the barn walls. Then there was Katie, who actually whistled while she shoveled, pausing now and then to pet one of the horses or coo at them in baby talk.

Emma slowed in front of the stall Katie cleaned, rolling in her lower lip as she studied her. The teen was a mystery, seemingly completely unaffected by the bad moods of the others in the camp. Her file was thin, her transgressions not nearly as severe compared to the other campers. If it didn't sound so ridiculous, she'd think Katie *wanted* to be at Camp Hope.

The ambitious little redhead had thrived the most on the rock climbing wall, too, reaching a height the other girls couldn't, though Stacy had certainly given it a solid try. Tonya struggled with the challenge, her feet slipping off the rocks and sending her swinging in her harness several times. She'd wobbled unsteadily once back on solid ground but quickly wrote it off to a fear of heights. Faith had pulled Emma aside, worrying that Tonya was lying since she hadn't mentioned her fear previously, but Emma chalked it up to the fact Tonya probably hadn't wanted to admit her phobia in front of the other girls. From what she'd seen at Camp Hope so far, saving face meant everything to these kids.

She could relate. Wasn't hiding her fears from both Max and Cody her own daily goal?

"How's Buttercup?"

Emma turned at the unfamiliar voice behind her. A pretty woman her own age strolled toward her, shiny chestnut hair pulled back in a low ponytail. She wore a denim jacket and carried a large duffel-style bag, and her eyes gave each horse she passed a cursory glance before she focused on Emma with a smile.

She assumed Buttercup was one of the horses but couldn't for the life of her figure out which one or why this woman cared. Was she a visiting parent? Max hadn't mentioned another counselor, even a part-time one. She hesitated. "Buttercup?" Made her think of cupcakes, which made her miss her favorite indulgence in Dallas. Funny how she hadn't missed anything else in the week-plus they'd lived in Broken Bend.

The woman gestured toward the last stall on the right. "The bay mare? Max said she was limping." She laughed. "Sorry, I always was guilty of getting right down to business. I'm Dr. Rachel Peters—veterinarian."

"Oh! Of course. I didn't realize something was wrong." Emma stepped aside for Rachel to pass her in the barn aisle, craning her head to make sure the girls were still working. "Go ahead. I'll go find Max."

"No." The doctor's expression darkened momentarily, and she cast a quick glance over her shoulder as if checking to make sure he wasn't already there. "That's totally not necessary."

Weird. Now an uneasy feeling crept through Emma's stomach. Maybe she'd read too many spy novels lately, but why would the vet *not* want the horse's owner to watch her perform a treatment? Something wasn't on the up-and-up. She might not know much about horses, but Emma knew enough about body language to know this woman was hiding something.

She followed her into Buttercup's stall. "Listen, this might not be my place, but I am on staff here right now, and I don't feel comfortable with this. I think I need to get Max." She crossed her arms, ready to argue further if necessary.

Rachel looked up from where she already knelt by Buttercup's left leg. Surprise highlighted her classically beautiful features. Then she laughed. "I guess that did sound sort of cryptic." She shook her head, and wisps of her hair fluttered against her face. "Max and I…we have a history of sorts. So I try to stay out of his way when I make house calls."

Another sick feeling spread through Emma's midsection, though she much preferred the first one to this. History. They'd dated. When? For how long? Had it been serious? A dozen questions vied for release at once, and Emma swallowed them all back. "I see." She didn't see, not really, and the fact left a bitter aftertaste in her mouth.

Rachel rubbed her hand down various parts of Buttercup's leg, and the horse continued to pull hay from her feeder with stubby lips as if nothing unusual were happening. "He and I go way back."

She nodded, though her heart shouted a contradiction. Not as far back as she and Max went.

Or did they?

Better yet, why did it matter?

"It's none of my business." Understatement of the year. But at the same time...Emma began easing backward out of the stall, dying to hear more, yet desperate to escape before she did. "I shouldn't have interfered."

Rachel lifted Buttercup's hoof and studied the shoe before carefully setting her leg back on the straw-covered ground. "It's sweet you're protective."

Protective? Of Max? Hardly. She'd just wanted to make sure some stranger wasn't harming his horses under her own nose. She opened her mouth to argue but Rachel continued, brushing her hair back from her face. "It's good to know he has someone looking out for him again. He's been brokenhearted before, you know." She knelt and rummaged through her bag.

Heat flushed a trail up Emma's neck and into her cheeks. She pressed her cold fingers against what surely had to be a telltale blush and sucked in a sharp breath. Brokenhearted. By her? By Rachel? Someone else?

Why did she have to care?

"By you?"

The words fluttered from her lips, and Emma bit back a gasp at having released them. Ever since she crossed the county line into Broken Bend, her self-control and restraint had been nearly nonexistent. She stifled words all day long in counseling sessions in Dallas. Why was she suddenly Ms. Loose Lips?

Rachel shook her head with a wistful smile. "Not me. That was the problem, actually. He was still hung up on someone from his past. Emma, I think was her name." She shrugged as if it didn't matter, but the two syllables rammed into Emma's ears like a fiery dart. Her chest caught and her ears flamed. Max still cared about her—after all those years. Even after her sudden desertion. So much so, he hadn't been able to move on.

She hadn't, either, though she hated to admit it was for the same reason.

But it was.

Emma braced one hand against the stall door to steady herself. His hug in the kitchen the other night had lent to the idea, but this—this was proof. Facts. More than just an emotional hug between two friends who used to be more.

Why, oh, why, did this new knowledge have to affect her so strongly? If anything, it twisted the knife of her secret deeper. Max had really been hurt by her leaving—even though she made the best choice she could at the time, it'd be so much easier to think he never cared. Never missed her. Never regretted anything.

Now what was she supposed to say? She could barely breathe, much less form a sentence.

Thankfully, Rachel didn't seem to expect an answer. "There's mild swelling in the left pastern. I'm going to have to do an X-ray." She stood and brushed her hands on the legs of her jeans. "We need to see what's going on in there."

Too bad the pretty veterinarian didn't have a machine that could tell Emma the same.

Max saw Dr. Peters's truck pull up from the window of his office, where he prayed between One4One sessions, and breathed a sigh of relief. Maybe now they could get to the bottom of what was hurting Buttercup. He shot a quick text to Tim to let him know he'd be right back before sending the next teen in, shoved his hat on his head and strode toward the barn.

Rachel preferred to treat the horses on her own unless there was a problem that required a decision on his part, and he couldn't really blame her. They'd dated a few times back when he worked for Brady, and while it'd been obvious she wanted to take things to the next level, he couldn't. Not honestly. Not without traces of Emma lingering in his heart. It just wasn't fair—Rachel deserved better.

So did Emma, for that matter. As she clearly

realized on her own the day she disappeared from his life.

But today, he wanted to see Rachel. He hadn't needed her at the ranch in almost six months, and it was a little ridiculous that they still acted like junior high kids at a dance—Awkward City. He was tired of hiding. It was time to be adults. Besides, he wanted to hear her opinion on Buttercup's leg firsthand since the mare had been perfectly fine last week. Hopefully it wasn't anything too dire— or expensive.

He entered the barn, welcoming the familiar scent of hay, leather and horseflesh, and inhaled deeply. It never failed to amaze him of all he'd accomplished in the past several years. If it hadn't been for Brady's kick in the hindquarters to get his own spread and put feet to his faith, he'd probably still be assisting his best friend at the Double C Ranch. But God was good, and through hard work and more than a little patience, Max had planted himself where he'd never imagined he'd be. And now, he couldn't imagine doing anything else.

All the more reason to keep atoning for the past. He owed God, big-time, for that much grace.

A horse nickered to his left, and he glanced over in time to see Stacy finishing up mucking Winston's stall. He smiled at her, but her lips barely quirked in response. Uh-oh, someone was getting tired of manure. At least she withheld any sarcasm, which was a major improvement. He made a mental note to praise her for that in their next session together.

To his right, he glimpsed Katie, whistling loudly as she groomed Max's best quarter horse, Remington, not even looking up as he strode past. Of all his campers, so far Katie had shown the least improvement—because she'd started out so far ahead of them all. Her file had only vaguely explained she needed to get away from negative influences, but he had yet to determine what all they were. She'd clearly wanted to come, as evidenced by her personal statement in the paperwork, but he still felt as if he was missing a piece of her story. It couldn't be anything that terrible, though, if she functioned so well at Camp Hope. He'd try to figure that out at their next One4One. As far as attitudes went, Katie won the award for Miss Congeniality.

His stomach twinged in automatic response as he glimpsed Emma at the far end of the barn, leaning against Buttercup's stall as she chatted with someone inside. Clearly she'd already met Dr. Peters. His step hitched as he drank in the sight of her. She looked good in his barn, though he'd already known that. Still, watching her stand there with arms loosely hanging over the door, one booted foot kicked up against the side, made her look as though she belonged. Once upon a time...

He opened his mouth to call a greeting, give the ladies fair warning of his approach, but not before Rachel's crystal clear voice rang from inside the stall.

"He was still hung up on someone from his past."

Oh. No. Max hesitated, unsure whether to hurry up or slow down. Interrupting would be embarrassing, but not as embarrassing as if Rachel actually said—

"Emma, I think was her name."

He should have hurried.

Max came to a stop, his boots scuffing on the concrete floor. They couldn't be discussing what he thought they were—could they? She and Emma had known each other all of, what, ten minutes? His chest tightened, and he drew a deep breath against it, trying to talk himself down. No big deal. Emma already knew he cared about her—at least a little, after that encounter in the kitchen last week. He'd hugged her in the middle of the night, for crying out loud, and told her he wished he'd have been there for her at her father's funeral. But what Rachel said took it a little further.

If he recognized that as a dude, he could only imagine how much further Emma was taking it.

His fears—hopes?—were confirmed as an immediate red flush crawled up her face. Her mouth opened and closed, as if she were unsure what to say, and she grabbed for the stall door frame.

He really wanted to be the one holding her up right now.

A warm feeling spread through his chest, returning his breath even as hers was apparently being stolen. His feelings mattered. The past few years still counted. Even hearing about it secondhand, her reaction proved it—she still felt something, too. If she were as indifferent toward him as she pretended, she'd have cared less at Rachel's admission.

Rachel came out of Buttercup's stall with her bag, her next words too low for Max to catch, and stopped abruptly as their gazes locked. Emma turned, and there they stood, an unlikely triangle, all eyes pointedly fixed on Max.

First he was jealous of the wood propping up Emma, now he was jealous of the horses that got to hide in their stalls. Not that he had any reason to be embarrassed—if anything, Rachel should be, for having slipped personal information about him to a near stranger.

Though, since they'd dated back in his womanizing, desperate-for-distraction days, he probably deserved it.

He adjusted his hat and grinned. "Ladies." He still had some charm left, somewhere. Not that it would affect either of those two. "How's Buttercup?"

Maybe if he pretended he hadn't heard, they could all save face. But denial had never been his specialty. He might have done a lot of things worse in the past, but lying was never his crutch.

He hadn't had anyone trying to keep him account-able in the first place until Emma. His dad couldn't care less what he did, and if Max told him flat out, he'd probably reach for another shot glass and toast him best wishes.

But they knew he'd heard. He could see it in the guilt clouding Rachel's eyes and the mortification lurking in Emma's.

"She needs an X-ray." Rachel jangled her truck keys as if in proof of her pending deed. "Was just headed to get the machine."

"And let me know?" An X-ray definitely fell under the unofficial doctor/client relationship they had going, though the question was more to distract from the tension radiating off Emma than from his own personal desire to find out.

"Of course." Rachel smiled, that gentle, practiced white smile she'd perfected over the years of hav-ing to break bad news to animal lovers.

But this time, Max knew the bad news had noth-ing to do with Buttercup.

"Need help?" She'd say no, but he had to ask anyway. Maybe she'd take pity on him—or Emma, at the least—and give them an excuse to delay the inevitable.

Nope. Rachel Peters owed Max Ringgold no fa-vors. Her smile deepened as she rushed past them. "I've got it."

Of course she did.

He couldn't resist. Not that he'd call it desperation but… "Are you sure? Emma or I could—"

Rachel stopped, back stiff, and slowly turned. "Emma?"

He pointed, and Emma ducked her head, turning even redder than before. In fact, she was downright burgundy. Clearly, he'd missed a step. He frowned. "Emma Shaver."

And then the pieces connected. Rachel had been talking to Emma earlier without knowing her name. Obvious, now, by the particular way she'd phrased her tell-all sentence. Too bad he hadn't caught that tiny detail before now. Talk about upping the embarrassment factor.

"I didn't know." Rachel's apologetic gaze was focused on Emma, not on him. Ouch. Probably some form of girl code he didn't get, either. "Sorry for… well, you know." She turned without meeting Max's eyes. "I'll just grab that machine now." Apparently the vet was still clinging to hope that Max hadn't overheard what she'd said. She hurried down the barn aisle and into the sunshine.

"You heard." Emma pointed out the obvious the second Rachel was out of earshot.

"I heard." He still couldn't lie—especially not to her eyes.

"So you and Rachel…Dr. Peters…" Emma gestured between him and the empty barn aisle behind him, her hand flopping listlessly like a fish on a bank. "You and she…"

He'd never seen such desperation for someone to fill in a blank. If it'd been anyone else, he'd have teased them a bit. Drawn it out. But she'd been through enough pain, he could tell. Talk about knowing the feeling. "We dated casually." He made sure to keep his voice down, despite the female campers being across the barn.

Instant relief drained the anxiety from her expression. "So it wasn't serious."

"Were you jealous?" He really didn't mean to say that out loud, but on second thought, maybe he did. Emma couldn't hold all the cards and leave him with nary a peek.

Her eyes flashed, and she crossed her arms over her chest, the defensive motion one he recognized all too well from her. "You're one to talk. You haven't dated anyone seriously since me."

"You're right."

The fight fled from her stance, and she took a tentative step toward him. "Why?"

"Why do you think, Emma?" She was so close. So familiar. He reached out and grazed her arm with his knuckles, her shirtsleeve soft under his touch. Man, that hurt deep. He hadn't realized until that fateful hug how badly he still craved her presence in his life. Craved her arms around him and her head on his shoulder. No one had ever fit like Emma had. But how could he tell her that without losing the tiny splinter of dignity he had left?

She shrugged, but the hope in her eyes left his

head spinning. She wanted him to tell her. But could he really hold his heart out for her to trample over a second time?

He yanked off his hat, ran his fingers through his hair and sighed before replacing it. "You're the one who left. Not me." That was about as straightforward as he could get. Without putting himself on a silver platter and saying "here." "Remember?"

The hope in her gaze morphed into something colder. "Oh, I remember, all right. I remember you—"

"Miss Shaver!" Katie's panicked cry sent a burst of adrenaline into Max's veins. He'd forgotten they weren't alone in the barn. Had the girls overheard Rachel's confession?

"Help!"

Either way, it didn't matter at the moment. He half caught Katie as she barreled toward them, straw stuck in her hair. His heart raced. "What's wrong?"

"Are you okay?" Emma grabbed for her hands, and Katie squeezed until her knuckles turned white.

"It's Tonya. She's on the floor next to Remington's stall." She panted for breath, eyes wide with fear. "I think she's unconscious."

Chapter Ten

Emma laid a cool washcloth on Tonya's head, gesturing for Katie to back up as she continued to bounce nervously. Apparently her burst of adrenaline over finding Tonya facedown in straw had yet to fade. "Careful now. Let her breathe."

She could say the same for Max, who didn't seem to care in the least that he was breaking his own rule about staying out of the female dormitory. He hovered over Tonya's bed, frowning down at her pale face, her dark hair stark against the white pillow.

"I still think we need to take her to the hospital."

Tonya lifted from the pillow, panic highlighting her expression. "No!"

He flinched, and even Katie backed up a step. No way could someone truly ill coax that strong of a tone. Emma raised her eyebrows at Tonya. Something was going on, for sure—had she been faking to get out of barn duties? She needed to run the idea by Max, but not in front of Tonya.

"Why not, Tonya? Afraid of needles?" Stacy spoke up from her spot on her bed across the room, and Tonya glared at her.

"That's enough." Max's voice left no room for disagreement—or sarcasm. Stacy slumped back against her pillow, but her smug smile didn't fade. Max caught Emma's eye and gestured with his head to the entryway area outside the dorm. He wanted to talk to her alone, too. About Tonya? Or their unfinished conversation?

She wasn't sure how she felt about the interruption earlier. One part grateful and two parts disappointed. She probably shouldn't have finished the sentence she'd been tempted to before Katie arrived panicking, but saying it would have felt *so* good. So relieving.

Sort of like justifying her decision and her secret for the hundredth time.

Great. How healthy was that? There she went again, trying to fix everyone around her while ignoring her own broken pieces. Too bad counseling oneself didn't work nearly as well. Though she knew what she'd tell herself if she were a patient— that truth was always better than lies. That anything worth hiding was worth telling. That relationships built on untruths would only crumble.

Saying it was easy. Living it, not so much. Especially when one's son could potentially go to jail based on the consequences of said truth.

And speaking of secrets, Tonya definitely had one.

Emma adjusted the washrag on the teen's forehead. She didn't feel warm, and her pulse had calmed. Maybe she really had faked it and knew an examination from a professional would rat her out. Still, she'd never been one to shirk out of chores before. If anything, Emma would have expected that behavior from Stacy—not Tonya.

At least the girls didn't seem to have heard the awkward conversation between the adults in the barn. Maybe Tonya passing out cold had been a blessing in one sense.

Max traded places by Tonya's side with Katie. "We'll be right back. Katie, keep this rag cool and come get us if something happens, okay?"

The eager redhead nodded and immediately stood guard and stared at Tonya as though she might fade away into the sheets if she so much as blinked. "Yes, sir."

Stacy snorted again, but Max let that one go. Emma followed him just outside the bedroom door and lowered her voice as she secured her stance by a potted fern. "So what are you thinking?" Best to let him lead the conversation, or she'd put them right back where they left off in the barn. She still couldn't decide if that would be good or bad.

"She might be faking. And if she is, I want her

busted." Max crossed his arms and sighed, the sleeves of his work shirt pulling taut across his biceps. "On the other hand, she says she just got hot shoveling and forgot to eat breakfast. It could be a blood sugar issue."

"I sat by her at breakfast. She only nibbled on an orange." Emma hesitated. "Come to think of it, I don't think she ate much at dinner last night."

Understanding began to slide across Max's face. "She's the only one that's been on a treadmill since we've been here, too. Have you ever seen her leave the table at a meal for the restroom?"

Surely he didn't think… "Eating disorder?" Emma frowned. "No. Well, maybe. I guess it's possible. What's in her file?"

"Nothing about that. But she's so thin. And I've seen it at this camp before." He rubbed his jaw, the day's stubble bristling under his fingers. "Let's keep a close eye on her."

"So, hospital or no hospital?" The heater in the dorm kicked on, sending a brush of warm air across Emma's shoulders. Still, she rubbed her hands up and down her arms, fighting a chill that wouldn't go away. If Tonya had a disorder, Emma should have picked up on it. She should have noticed long before the girl fainted. What good was she even doing here?

"I'm not going to make her go this minute. But I do have to call her parents and see what they advise. Legally, I can't ignore this whether Tonya thinks she's fine or not." Max leaned against the door, his voice nearly a whisper to avoid being overheard from inside. "If they don't insist, then we'll see what happens tomorrow. I'll make her go if she passes out again."

"Will her parents come get her early? Is that even allowed?"

"It's a disruption, one we try to avoid at all costs. Anytime a parent has to intervene in the program, it typically halts progress."

A second, more intense shiver skirted up her spine. "And I'm *not* intervening?"

His mouth opened, but Emma pushed ahead, panic driving her words past her control. He'd just said it himself—her nightmare, brought verbally to life. Fear clouded her vision. "I'm Cody's parent first, Max. Before I'm these girls' counselor or your lifesaver or whatever it was you called me when I agreed to this whole crazy thing." She jabbed her finger at his chest. "I'm his *mother.*"

He wrapped his hand around her pointed finger and gently, but firmly, lowered her hand. Her breath caught, his touch sending small sparks up to her elbow and combating the chill leftover from cold truth. "I know who you are, Emma Shaver."

And there they were. Back in the barn, with a thousand unspoken words hovering between them. But which ones to speak? And would it accomplish anything other than relieving a bit of stress and then leaving her drenched in regret? She was tired of regret. Tired of wondering. Tired of doubting. Would she ever make it through the rest of the month?

Would Cody?

A sob began to work its way up her chest, and she swallowed it back. She couldn't be that vulnerable in front of Max. It just wasn't right. Not after everything they'd been through. No, she needed walls. Brick ones. Big, tall, brick ones.

"If I thought you were hindering Cody, I wouldn't have let you stay." Max's confident tone spiked through her fears and left her hoping for... well, hope.

"Are you sure?" Her heart thundered. "Maybe you're just blinded to the facts because of need."

"Don't pull that textbook stuff out with me." His smile tempered his words. "I would never sacrifice a teenager because of a camp need. The campers are why I'm here."

"Then what would you have done if I'd said no?" Emma realized suddenly he hadn't let go of her hand, yet she couldn't force herself to pull it away. She wanted him to let go first.

This time.

"If you had said no, God would have sent someone else." He squeezed her fingers, and she squeezed back as if on autopilot. "He's sort of on the side of Camp Hope, you know."

She really didn't know whose side God was on, except that it probably wasn't hers. But no need to get into theology while they had a potentially bulimic girl, a lame horse and a camp full of teenagers needing their supper to deal with. She risked a glance into his face, and her heart clenched at his eyes, so similar to Cody's, gazing down at her with such sincerity. Such honesty. Such compassion.

Where had Max Ringgold gone? The man she knew from days ago was nothing like this. That man had been hard enough to walk away from—but this one…

How could she walk away a second time?

She tugged her hand free. "I'll keep a closer watch on Tonya. I promise."

"This wasn't your fault." Max's arm hung limp at his side as if he didn't know what to do with his suddenly empty hand. She could relate, so she hooked her thumbs into her back pockets. "You do know that, right?"

Not her fault. That's what everyone told her about Cody, too, and what she often told parents of wayward children she saw in counseling. But wasn't a piece of it her fault? She had to be responsible to a degree—even if it was the single mistake of going against God's Word and sleeping with Cody's father when she knew better. Knew he wasn't legit. Knew he wouldn't change for her.

But he had changed, and maybe the fact that it *wasn't* for her was what hurt worst of all.

"These teens ultimately have to make their own choices. That goes for Tonya—and Cody." Max's fingers brushed her shoulder, and she leaned into the warmth before easing away from the touch that so easily got her in trouble. "Emma, you have to believe me."

His words hit her heart but didn't penetrate, like an arrow flung at a target without enough force to stick. "I know you think that."

"It's true."

Maybe it was. Maybe it wasn't *her* fault, so much as it was his. Max Ringgold, for however much he'd crossed over to the good side, had once very much occupied the darkness. Weren't bad boy genes hereditary? The Bible even talked about the sins of the father being passed down. Maybe Cody didn't have a chance at all because of his very DNA. Maybe his future was already determined in the negative. Didn't all of it—the vandalism, the fighting, the rebellion—come so naturally to her son?

She'd seen the same thing in his father.

And if she looked really hard—in herself.

"I'm going to go check on Tonya." She drew a ragged breath before pushing open the dormitory door behind him. "We're done here."

She was getting really good at walking away from him. Max stayed in the entryway after the door shut behind her, wondering if he should follow.

Or walk away for good.

But the only way to walk away from Emma

Shaver was physically. And he wasn't leaving Camp Hope, and for the time being, neither was she. He somehow had to find a way to stick out this arrangement he'd plopped them both into and move forward for the sake of the kids. This was about the campers—not him. His struggles and dreams and desires were not at stake, but an entire dormful of teenagers' were, including one potentially sick young girl who needed his attention and support. Not his half effort and attention because he was so distracted by Emma.

The heater shut off, leaving a heavy silence surrounding the entryway. He rubbed his temples beneath the rim of his cowboy hat and stared down at the linoleum squares beneath his boots. He should have known. And maybe he had. Maybe God had sparked the idea and arranged for Emma to fill the temporary need of counseling—but hadn't his own heart jumped at the opportunity to spend regular time with her again? He'd bit that bullet a lot more eagerly than he'd tried to convince himself at first.

Hopefully he hadn't jumped ahead of God. He was so used to lingering behind the Lord, dragging his heels and denying his purpose in starting Camp Hope for so long, that he wasn't sure if he'd recognize what it meant to run ahead, to carve his own path and hope it was the same one God wanted him to walk.

Maybe he wasn't supposed to be anything more for Emma right now than a counselor to her son.

That would have to be enough—regardless of how good she felt in his arms. Regardless of how his heart ached to atone for the past.

Regardless of how the sight of her walking away from him made him feel like a helpless, love-struck teenager once again.

But they had to come to some kind of truce. He and Emma couldn't keep playing emotional relay, passing the baton of the past back and forth in heated arguments. He glanced toward the door, wishing he could barrel back inside and demand Emma come settle this once and for all. He was sick of elephants crowding their time together and wreaking havoc on his memories.

The door opened, and his heart leaped before realizing it was Stacy. Then it jumped again for a different reason. Had something else happened to Tonya?

"She okay?" His tone sounded more clipped than he meant for it to, and it seemed Stacy picked up on it, as well. Her posture stiffened.

"She's fine. Trust me." Stacy smirked.

Smug. Too smug. Max narrowed his eyes. "What do you know?"

Her grin faded, and real anxiety flashed across her expression before morphing back into neutral. "Nothing, I swear."

Yeah, right. "No lying at Camp Hope."

Stacy snorted. "You do realize that's a dumb rule? Everyone lies. And how will you even know?"

She crossed her arms, all rebellion. And probably a bit of jealousy over the attention her roommate was receiving.

Max's spirits sagged. They'd come so far, and now... He withheld the sigh begging for release. "Call it a gift." Too bad he'd never seen the truth in Emma's eyes before she deserted their relationship years ago. He could have saved himself the pain and embarrassment of all the unanswered calls and emails. Could have avoided the hope that she just got busy at school and would be home for Christmas. Or Valentine's. Or Easter. But the holidays passed, and then spring, and then the entire summer.

He'd never seen it coming. And he would never make that mistake in misreading someone again.

Starting with Tonya—and the stubborn girl standing before him.

"I can tell when someone is lying." He leaned down slightly and peered right into Stacy's eyes. She backed up a step, brow furrowed, as one hand nervously reached up to wind blond strands around her finger. "Trust *me*."

For a moment, it looked as though she might believe him. Panic took over once again, and her lips parted. But instead of revealing truth, she slammed the mask securely back in place and turned her mouth into a sarcastic grin. She shot a pointed look at the dorm behind her leading to Tonya. "Guess we'll see about that."

* * *

Emma sat at the long kitchen table inside the main house later that night, legs crossed in her favorite pair of lounge pants. A mug of hot chocolate that Mama Jeanie had graciously prepared for her sat at her side, while Tonya's, Katie's and Stacy's files were spread open before her.

She slowly flipped through the pages as a carved wooden cuckoo clock ticked above her head, reminding her she'd been here for a while already and didn't have much to show for it. She'd been able to get away from the dorm for a bit since Faith had come to stay the night as backup for Tonya, who had been excused from the rest of the evening's activities. Max told her, though, if she couldn't keep up the next morning, she had an E.R. trip in her immediate future—even if her parents had allowed her to skip it today.

She turned another page in Tonya's file, hoping to find insight that could point her in the right direction. It was weird looking at Max's careful, handwritten notes in the margins. Too bad she couldn't get a true glimpse of Cody's file. When she'd gotten close enough to be tempted earlier, all she'd seen was the contact page of Cody's information, before her conscience caught up and she'd shut the folder and put it away. She really wanted to read what Max had written during their counseling sessions, and gauge any of Cody's potential progress for herself. She was so desperate to know what to expect when they went home in a few weeks. Was the fact that Max wasn't keeping her up-to-date a bad sign? Or just protocol?

Her eyes lingered on the stack of files again. But no, she couldn't interfere like that. It wasn't her place, and those choices wouldn't exactly draw her closer to her son. Besides, she'd already seen more than she knew what to do with—a typo. And not just any typo, but one regarding Cody's birthday.

Her stomach flipped like it had when she'd seen it. A blessing in disguise? Now even if Max suspected, he wouldn't be able to prove it….

Or was it just one more item to add to her guilt-ridden list?

The desk lamp she'd borrowed from the living area cast a dim glow across her paperwork. She picked up her mug of cocoa and swirled it gently, watching the marshmallows float in an easy circle by the rim and wishing this whole situation hadn't grown so complicated. Somehow, she'd lost control of her own son, yet been put in charge of three incredibly different young ladies—not to mention been dropped straight into the daily presence of the exact man she'd gone to great lengths to avoid for over a decade.

Who said God didn't have a sense of humor?

If she weren't so jaded, she'd examine that a little further. She didn't really believe God was laughing at her or had arranged these circumstances at her expense. Rather, she believed in punishment.

Judgment for sins. Living out the consequences of bad choices. Hadn't she done that her whole life? She'd sacrificed so much to keep her pregnancy a secret, and then to keep Cody's father's identity a secret—because she should. She deserved to pay for her mistakes. As the saying went—she'd made her bed.

But had those sacrifices cost too much?

"Marshmallows can't talk, you know."

She jerked, cocoa spilling onto her hand. Of course Max knew she'd been there, since he'd gotten the files for her earlier that evening. But she hadn't expected him to come hang out—especially not after their exchange that afternoon in the dorm.

He grabbed a dishrag that was folded by the sink and tossed it to her, his lips turned up in amusement. "Sorry. You were just staring into your cup so hard I figured you were expecting an answer."

If only it were that simple. "It's okay. Just daydreaming." At night. About him.

And his son.

She dabbed her hand dry and tossed the towel at the far end of the table. Too bad she couldn't throw away her worries as easily.

He pulled up the chair beside her, turning it backward before straddling it. Clad in faded jeans and a college sweatshirt, sans hat, he looked way too much like the Max from the old days. The one who could charm his way into her heart with a single look. The one who'd stolen a lot more than he'd ever given back.

The one who once had convinced her he wanted a life with her.

"Find any hidden treasures in there?" He pointed to Tonya's file, and she closed it before passing it over.

"If you mean explanations, no." She brushed her hair out of her eyes and shifted to face him, suddenly regretting the decision to wear yoga pants. "We'll have to play it out."

"I figured. I've read all the campers' files several times, and I just don't know. At least we're watching closely now."

"Better late than never, huh?" She offered a half smile, but he returned it with that serious gaze that still seemed so foreign to her—and still sent shivers over her skin.

"I agree." His heavy-lidded eyes narrowed thoughtfully as he studied her, and an impish grin quirked the side of his mouth.

Her stomach clenched, and she slowly slid her mug away. "We're not talking about Tonya anymore, are we?"

Chapter Eleven

"I need you."

She stared at Max as if sitting motionless could somehow make his words visible. Surely she didn't hear him correctly. "What did you say?"

He didn't blink, just held her gaze with those steady eyes. Those eyes that always reminded her of hot chocolate with a little too much milk. "I need you."

Oh, wait, they'd done this before. She relaxed slightly in her chair, futilely attempting to calm her erratic heartbeat. "Right. You mean, here. At the camp." She let out a breath. "I know. Trust me, I wouldn't be here if you didn't." Hadn't they said that already? Why did he have to keep bringing it up? He probably thought she needed more affirmation after today's episode with Tonya, but he was taking it a little too far.

"No." He reached for her hand resting on the table and threaded his fingers through hers. An immediate shock wave radiated up her arm, and she tensed but didn't pull away. "I mean, I need you. I need to be around you. I need…" His voice trailed off and he glanced down at their joined hands. "This."

No. He wasn't. He couldn't. "Max." His name left her lips like honey dripping from a spoon. Sweet and achingly slow. She couldn't conceal the emotion he still generated inside her. But this couldn't happen. Not for a hundred reasons.

Especially not for one.

"I miss you."

She missed him, too. And what did that say about her? She missed the man who represented her biggest regret in life. Not Cody, of course. He wasn't a regret, even in spite of the heartache of the past few years.

But Max—big regret. Big heartache.

What was wrong with her? She was worse than a moth to a flame. At least the moths didn't know better. She did—and was still tempted.

"I know it's impossible." He held on tightly to her fingers, as if fighting the inevitable, and finally broke eye contact to rub his thumb over her hand. "But if it wasn't…I'd be tempted to do this." He lifted her hand and brushed his lips against her knuckles.

Chills raced down her arms as heat—and memories—warmed her heart. His lips moved up to her wrist, sending tingles into her shoulder.

"Or this." In one fluid motion, he scooted his chair a foot closer to hers, leaned over and cupped her neck with one hand, thumb grazing the side of her cheek.

She closed her eyes, knowing what was next. This was wrong. So wrong. But it was Max. So familiar. She couldn't think. Couldn't breathe, much less form a coherent thought. When was the last time he'd kissed her?

Oh. Yeah.

She jerked away as if burned, nearly tilting her chair backward. "No. No!"

"I heard you." Max held up both hands in surrender, still close enough to touch but obeying her protest. "I'm sorry."

He'd tried to start it up again. And she'd almost let him.

It was almost enough.

Almost.

"It wouldn't be right." His words came out a statement but left a clear question mark ending. "You're working here."

"I'm working here." She parroted numbly, unable to back away any farther from his magnetism but knowing if she didn't, she might very well find herself pulling the same move on him. "I work here." There, that was a reason he could understand. A reason she could actually share, anyway.

"You work here." He repeated it back, nodding,

until the sly charm she never could resist filled his eyes. "For three more weeks. Give or take."

Three weeks. A lifetime. Same difference. With Max, time stopped and sped up and rewound and did all sorts of crazy things she couldn't control. And that was the problem—with Max, she had no control. Never did.

And unfortunately, not a lot had changed, because if a year ago—six months ago, or even a week ago—someone had told her she'd have Max Ringgold's hands in her hair, she'd have laughed in their face at the absurdity.

God really, really had a sense of humor.

She needed control back. Not just with Max—with her life. With her son. With the family she'd sacrificed for and fought to create.

A family Max didn't fit into. Not yet. Not like this.

She had to resist.

She dug deep, closing her eyes and bringing back to life a box of memories she alternated between, regularly reliving and regularly shutting out. Max with a baggie of white powder. Max, getting yet another DUI from the sheriff, who threatened to tell Emma's parents on her if he ever saw her with "that riffraff" again. Max, trading cash for drugs with a local gang banger two weeks after promising her he'd been clean.

There. She could do it.

"Three weeks or three years—it's not happening." She opened her eyes and steeled herself against the hurt radiating from his posture.

A muscle worked in his jaw, and despite knowing better, she desperately wanted to touch it. Feel the rough bristle of a permanent five o'clock shadow under her fingers. Graze that dimple in his chin. She knew, instinctively, she had one last chance. He hadn't shut her out yet, she could tell by his expression. She could undo her last words—if she spoke now.

But what would that accomplish? More pain? More mistakes? More daily reminders that she'd screwed up and had been paying for it ever since? Maybe he'd be a good influence on Cody. But once he knew the truth—it'd change everything. He'd never look at her that way again, and worse yet, he could resent Cody for her choice. Resent them both.

Her heart couldn't break over Max Ringgold a second time without permanently disassembling.

Besides, she couldn't risk Cody being kicked out of the program. Smack-dab in the middle of his last-chance before juvie was not the time to correct a mistruth he'd believed his entire life. Not without doing damage none of them could repair in time.

The clock ticked a rhythm above their heads. Max raised his eyebrows, waiting. One more try. One last heartbeat. She held her breath.

And the cuckoo chirped the hour.

* * *

Max ignored the crack spreading across his heart, ignored the desire seeping through his chest, and plastered on the best fake smile he could muster. "Truce, then." He held out his hand, and Emma shook it, wariness holding her expression hostage. He didn't blame her, after what he'd just pulled. What had he been thinking, going for broke like that?

He let her hand go immediately, despite the cry of his instincts to hold on longer, and stood to straighten his chair. He dragged it several feet away, back to its rightful place, and reminded himself that from now on, this was his rightful place, too. Where he belonged—away from Emma. A respectful distance, anyway. She'd made her choice.

A man could only get kicked while he was down so many times, and twice was enough.

Emma stood, too, as if she was afraid he was forcing her to leave. Hardly. He needed her here— for the camp. He'd just be sure to keep his personal issues out of it. "You can go back to your files. No need to run off."

Again.

"I think I'm done for the night." She stared at the paperwork, looking young and overwhelmed in wrinkled sweatpants and a purple hooded sweatshirt. He drew his eyes away from the strands of blond hair skimming her shoulders. "There's nothing there."

Oh, there was.

Just not in Tonya's file.

"We'll see how she does in the morning. In the meantime…" Max hesitated, gripping the back of the dining room chair in front of him.

Emma crossed her arms. "The truce."

"The truce." He nodded. "Friends?"

Surprise flickered across her pale face, and he'd have given his right arm to know why. Did she really think he was an all or nothing kind of guy now? That their history forever determined their future? There was always room for pages to be rewritten. If he didn't believe in fresh starts, what kind of leader was he, anyway?

She rolled in her bottom lip, just like she'd always done when she was younger. Just like he'd seen Cody do a dozen times while at the camp. "Friends."

Relief flushed through his body. It wasn't what he really wanted, but at least the awkwardness could be shoved behind them now. They could move forward and focus together on what was most important—the kids.

"Then I'm going to need your help." He motioned for her to sit again, and she quickly obeyed as if eager to press forward with their new relationship. They needed to cement the decision, for sure, before the sun rose and reality doused them in an unforgiving light. "I really want to brainstorm a few new ideas for the campers. I'm not getting through to some of them like I expected to by now."

"Is Cody one of them?" Her brow puckered, and she tapped a nervous rhythm with her pencil.

"Don't worry about who." He offered what he hoped was a reassuring smile, but he couldn't discuss Cody right now. It was too soon—and not fair. He couldn't do that with the other campers and their parents, so he wouldn't start breaching confidentiality now. Besides, Emma was too anxious over it—wrong mindset on her part. There was still a long road to walk.

For both of them.

"I'd like your help, especially with some project ideas for the girls. These kids need to work hard, but they need to have fun." He patted Tonya's files. "They need to see they can have a good time without abusing substances or breaking the law."

"But isn't the point of the camp to learn discipline and responsibility? Learn how to respect authority?" Her frown lingered, though interest had sparked her gaze at the mention of fun.

"Of course. Don't you think we've been doing that?"

She hesitated, then snorted. He took that as a yes. She was probably remembering the early hours, the structured eating schedule, the punishment for forgotten manners, cursing and fighting, the strict rules about free time, the obstacle course that nearly did the group in...

"So, you'll help me?" He hated how much it mattered that she not turn down this small gesture.

She nodded slowly, eyes appraising him. He tried to look stoic. No more tricks. He wouldn't take advantage of their chemistry again—even if the air sizzled like a campfire every time he got within three feet of her. He tried to convey that honest message with his own gaze, not surprised in the least that they could still read each other so easily. After all they'd been through…

"I'll help."

"Great." His breath escaped in a rush of air. "Tomorrow, then." He wanted to shake her hand again. No, scratch that. He wanted to kiss her good-night.

Time to cowboy up and face facts. He stood, scooted their chairs in, gathered the files, held the door for her and smiled like a gentleman.

The entire time Emma stomped over his heart on her way to the dorms.

Emma slapped her alarm clock as it buzzed, and then curled into a stretch, wishing she could crash for another eight hours. She'd lost a lot of sleep over the years because of Max Ringgold, and last night was no exception. His words kept replaying in her head, a record stuck on repeat with an incessant message.

Max still wanted her.

The fact brought more nightmares than dreams, and she fell asleep too close to dawn.

Suddenly, she sat up in bed, fully awake. Today was Tonya's testing period. Would she pass?

Tonya's bed was empty, the covers pulled up and her pillow fluffed. Emma frowned. A quick glance confirmed Katie and Stacy were still asleep, sprawled haphazardly across their sheets as only teens could do. Where was Tonya?

Grabbing her slippers in one hand and her toiletry case in the other, she padded toward the entryway for the bathrooms, heart thumping with unease. If Tonya was still sick, she wouldn't be up and about so early.

But what if they were on to her, and she'd panicked? Done something really crazy, like run away?

Sort of ridiculous to think a teenager would make her bed before attempting jailbreak, but it was just as ridiculous for someone as beautiful as Tonya to think she needed to starve herself to look attractive. Teenagers sometimes did crazy things to feel loved and accepted.

Emma was a poster child for that particular motto.

She ducked back as the dormitory door swung open, nearly clipping her slipper-clad toes. "Oh, sorry." Tonya grimaced at the near miss, but the vibrancy in her complexion and the simple fact that she was there, dressed in a purple robe with her hair freshly braided, lifted Emma's spirits.

She fought the urge to hug her. "You're looking better." Understatement of the year. Compared to her pallor yesterday after the barn incident, Tonya looked runwayworthy once again.

"Feeling better." Tonya smiled, and it seemed sincere enough. Either she'd taken some acting classes overnight, or whatever had plagued her had passed. Maybe it'd been nothing more than low blood sugar, after all.

She just really hoped it hadn't been lies. Max didn't do well with those.

Ironically.

"Ready for breakfast?" Emma lowered her voice so not to wake the other girls, though they'd be getting up in about ten or fifteen minutes anyway. "I think Mama Jeanie said something yesterday about pancakes."

A brief shadow flickered across Tonya's expression before the grin returned. "Sounds great."

Did it? She made a mental note to watch Tonya's eating habits closely.

"I'm glad you're on the mend, but if you feel off today at all, let me know." She tried to mimic the firm tone Max used that worked so easily on the teens. "We want you to be okay." She tried to hold Tonya's gaze, show her compassion, but the younger girl dodged it, shaking off further inquiry.

"I'm fine. I promise." She lifted one slim shoulder in a shrug and fiddled with the satiny ties of her robe.

Max's famous line ran through her mind in protest—*no lying at Camp Hope*—but she swallowed the words. The girls heard that often enough. They needed to trust Emma, not take her as a nag. They already had moms—well, most of them. They needed a teammate, someone they could trust while they grew and healed.

But healing never began without first acknowledging the wound.

Her thoughts turned back to Max as Tonya slipped past and began rummaging through her dresser. Emma thought she'd healed from their fling—no, it was more than that. Labeling it as such was clearly a defense mechanism she'd concocted years ago. She had to start being honest with herself, just like Max had been honest last night.

A heavy sense of realization settled in her stomach, as hard and unforgiving as a boulder. But she couldn't avoid it any longer. This particular truth didn't seem able to set her free, but rather, it confined her in the same chains she'd struggled against for years.

She still needed him, too.

Chapter Twelve

Cody Shaver might not have his mom's eyes, but he'd definitely inherited her uncanny ability to clam up at the slightest hint of a breached wall.

Max shifted in his office chair, ignoring the squeak of the fake leather and trying not to show the frustration building within his chest. They'd been making such progress in their One4One— two-plus weeks into the program now, and he'd gotten through to Cody about his behavior. He'd also been able to praise the kid for several well-done chores and even secured a promise to apologize to Jarvis for the fighting incident.

Then he'd asked Cody about his dad, and the boy's jaw clamped tighter than Nugget with Brady's favorite cowboy hat.

"So your father…"

Face pale against his black T-shirt, Cody shook his head, a dull ache in his eyes. "I already told you. I don't know who he is."

That was so not like Emma. A blank name on Cody's paperwork under father? How could she not know? No, Emma knew, and didn't want to say. Why?

Unless… A wild thought crossed his mind, so wild he felt ridiculous even considering it. But the timing… He turned Cody's file to check the kid's birthday and started a desperate backward count down in his head.

Cody slumped in his seat. "All I know is he was some jerk who left my mom when she was pregnant and never came back."

His eyes lingered on the numbers before him, and his heart swam in an odd mixture of disappointment and amusement, all at the same time. The timing was impossible, by almost a year. Who was he kidding? Emma hadn't thought twice about him after she left.

But this wasn't about him.

No, this was about a boy who had been abandoned by his own father before he could even meet him and clearly carried those wounds around on his shoulders.

And Emma—he hurt for her. Even though she'd clearly gotten involved with someone quickly after she left Max, no one deserved what she'd been through. What she and Cody had been through together.

Max drew in a deep breath, determined to put Emma aside for the moment and talk about Cody's issues alone. "Let's talk about your dad for a minute. How knowing that he never came back makes you feel."

A warning flashed in Cody's eyes, indicating a hot button, and Max hesitated. He didn't want to start a fight or war of the wills, but he had to reach through the shield Cody still held and get to the source of the boy's hurt. Once there, Max could help him figure out how to process the behaviors Cody felt and decide if he needed to be referred to a professional. More than half of the teens that left Camp Hope received a referral, which made Max sick inside. The teens' parents clearly cared enough to bring them to the facility, but they never realized how much of a part of the overall problem they often were themselves.

Workaholism. Alcoholism. Perfectionism. Transferring fears of guilt, rejection and failure onto their kids. Without the right coping skills, the teens ran to whatever distractions or pleasures they could get to the quickest. It was sad.

And it made Max wonder if he'd be better off never bringing his own children into the world someday. Brady teased him about finding the right woman already so their kids could play together one day, but he didn't know. His own father had screwed him up—and it was solely by the grace of God that Max had escaped the destructive cycle. He had no guarantees he would be able to keep it up.

"I don't feel anything. I'm fine." Cody crossed his arms.

"I understand this isn't a fun topic." Max shifted forward in his chair, having chosen to sit beside Cody rather than let the desk separate them. "But it's probably more important than you realize. If you can just tell me a little about how—"

"No!" Cody stood up, skinny chest heaving, cheeks red and eyes glassy. Clearly, he was fighting a losing battle with tears. "I don't have to, and I don't want to."

Time to retreat. But they wouldn't end the session in such a negative place. Max gestured for Cody to sit back down. He obeyed, grudgingly, his eyes as wary as a doe's in November, and fixed his gaze somewhere near the potted plant behind Max's chair.

Fortress closed. But he'd dealt with worse. There was always a drawbridge if you looked hard enough. "There's one more thing we need to talk about today, then you can go on to your chores." He pressed on, pretending not to watch as Cody slowly regained control of his emotions and unclenched his jaw. "How are you doing with your mom being here on campus?"

"I hardly ever see her. So it's fine." He rolled his eyes. "Wish she'd avoid me this much at home."

Ouch. That would have cut right through Emma's jean jacket and straight into her heart. Max struggled to hide his surprise at the boy's choice of words. "You feel smothered at home?" Well, didn't every teen?

"I guess. I mean, she's just always on me, wanting to know what I'm doing and where I'm going and who I'm with."

He hid a smile. That just meant she was doing her job as a mom—and doing it well. "Don't you think that maybe some of your past choices have given her a reason to ask a lot of questions?"

He flushed red. "Yeah."

"So give her some slack, okay? Here's a secret about parents." He leaned forward as if he were about to reveal the mother lode of teenaged treasure.

Cody pretended indifference, but his eyes lit with interest.

"The more truth you tell them, the more they back off." He knew that was the case more often than not, and he could easily see how Emma's personality fed into that. If Emma could trust Cody again, she'd be more comfortable giving him some space. And teen boys needed a degree of space— he could remember the hormones and the struggle that came with being thirteen. It was a balancing act, and Emma and Cody were about to topple off the wire if something didn't change.

"You think so?" Cody squinted with uncertainty.

"It's a fact. You need to show your mom she can trust you. And she can't trust you until you make good decisions in front of her. Be responsible, that sort of thing."

"Like, doing my chores the first time she harps on me?"

Max rubbed his jaw, briefly hiding the smile he couldn't contain. There were moments like this every so often that popped up and reminded him that Cody was only thirteen—his youngest camper, and in so many ways, still a child. It brought comfort—that maybe Cody wasn't too far gone after all—yet also, unease. Kids in Cody's position didn't need to be naive or gullible about themselves, either.

"Yes, like that. And also, like, not sneaking out of the house to vandalize your school." He hardened his pointed stare, and Cody ducked his head.

Mission accomplished. He'd gotten through. Now to move forward.

"You're doing really well here." He waited until Cody glanced up at him, and smiled, willing the boy to relax and not shut down again. "I'm proud of your accomplishments."

The straight line of his shoulders sagged slightly, and his eyebrows perked. "So I'm going to pass?"

"That's up to you." Max shrugged, the casual move a contradiction to the urgency in his gut. He still wasn't certain why Cody passing the program mattered so much to him personally. He cared about all his campers, and it ate at him the few times he'd had to send teenagers home early for consistently destructive behavior. He couldn't save them all, and he knew that.

But he really wanted to save Cody.

It had to be his ties to Emma, which hopefully Cody was still unaware of. It'd be hard for him to trust Max if he felt Max was more on his mom's side than his own.

Which was true in some ways—but not necessarily in others. He knew no parent was perfect, but until he got the whole story, it was hard to determine where the blame really lay. Each teen was ultimately responsible for his own actions, but if it were evident they'd had a disadvantage from birth, Max tried to address it with the parents and even the courts, if needed.

Cody had to pass. For his own sake, and for Emma's. Max would do all he could to help him, but he wouldn't cut corners or let the boy off without earning it. Enabling would only land Cody in jail one day. "You'll pass if you keep doing the hard work."

Cody plucked at the intentional hole in the knee of his jeans. "I've almost nailed the rope swing." His voice lifted with a thin layer of optimism, though Max could sense the trepidation still under the surface.

"You'll get it." He nodded with confidence, wishing he could follow Cody around and verbally build the boy up even after he left camp. He thrived under compliments. Did Emma realize? He made a mental note to tell her. "But I don't mean just physical hard work."

Cody sighed hard enough to rustle the stack of papers on Max's desk. "I know."

"Next One4One." His tone didn't elicit an argument, and thankfully, Cody didn't try. He stood, inviting Cody to do the same, and walked him to the office door. "You're doing good, man. You know that, right?"

He stopped just outside the door, eyes focused somewhere near his boots. "I guess."

Under-confidence was just as bad, if not worse, than overconfidence. It seemed lately it was a lot easier to knock down than build up. "Just do me a favor. Don't stop the process." He wanted to jump inside Cody and fill whatever void lingered. From his father. From his lack of connection with his mom. From God. The teen years were scary enough in the most ideal of conditions—and Cody's situation was far from ideal.

As was Emma's.

When Cody finally lifted his head and nodded, blond hair falling over his eyes in a cowlick he'd been fighting since his first day on the ranch, Max drew a sharp intake of breath. For a minute, he'd seen something so familiar in Cody's expression, it'd been like looking in a mirror.

Must be his own past saying hi to Cody's present. How many times had Max felt the exact same way Cody looked? Confused. Lost. Trapped in his own skin.

More determined to help the boy than ever, Max shut the door behind him with a solid thump and briefly rested his forehead against it. He still needed to find out what made Cody tick.

Which meant one thing.

He needed to talk to Emma.

Emma didn't know which had her more on edge—the constant awareness of everything Tonya did or didn't put in her mouth, or the fact that Stacy stood armed and ready ten paces to her left with a bow and arrow.

Rubber tipped, but still. Good thing she didn't have an apple on her head.

Emma pulled the sleeves of her hoodie down farther over her hands to warm them as Luke and one of the part-time counselors jogged back and forth between campers, demonstrating the proper technique of drawing back the arrow on the bow. The goal was to let it fly toward the stacked hay bales so many yards downwind. It looked impossibly far to her.

"What's the point of this whole archery thing?" Emma snagged Max's shirtsleeve as he strolled past, his face relaxed and bronze in the sunshine streaming across the open field. The afternoon breeze rustled the hair under his cowboy hat, and he glanced down at her hand on his arm before she abruptly removed it. Definitely had to remember her no-touching rule, or she'd permanently walk around feeling as if she'd been zapped in the hand.

"It's a group competition. I'm teaching them the value of teamwork and encouragement." His grin widened. "Plus, it's fun."

Teamwork and encouragement. Right. Emma just hoped it wouldn't teach a new vehicle for violence. They weren't exactly in the presence of a bunch of Maid Marians.

"Trust me." Max squeezed her shoulder before moving past her. "You'll see." He winked, and she was left torn between focusing on the butterflies stirred by his touch and snorting over his request to trust him.

Either inevitably proved useless, so she focused on her girls instead.

Beside her, Katie bounced excitedly, waiting for her turn, while Tonya stood coolly with arms crossed, no doubt concerned that archery wouldn't go much better for her than the obstacle course. Those two were on Luke's team, while Jarvis, Stacy and Cody had been placed on the other male counselor's team.

"Archers ready!" Max clapped his hands. "Luke, you're up. You won the toss."

Luke's team slapped high fives, while he quickly bent and went over a few reminders to Katie. "You're up, Red."

She blushed at the nickname but seemed to enjoy

the cheers from her group. Emma slowly relaxed. Apparently the team idea was a stroke of genius, because even those that had mocked the competition previously were suddenly on board, shouting encouragement to Katie.

Her first shot went high, over the bales, but her second nailed just to the right of the target's bull's-eye. She struck a sassy pose before passing the bow to the boy in line behind her.

From Max's team, Jarvis drew back the arrow and landed two solid hits to the target, though not as close as Katie's near bull's-eye. He handed their team's bow off to Cody and sneered. "Good luck. You'll need it."

Emma took a step forward before catching herself, then looked to see if Max had caught the exchange. If he had, he wasn't letting on. Frustration stirred, but she kept her feet firmly in place—despite the urge to march over to Cody's side and intervene.

Then a cold wave of suspicion doused her anger. Was this the kind of thing Cody dealt with at school every day? If he were the subject of constant teasing and tormenting due to his size and the perspective of being an easy target, no wonder he had so much pent-up aggression. No wonder he kept trying to prove himself to his peers, earn acceptance the wrong way.

She stared at her son as if she'd never seen him before.

Maybe she hadn't.

Cody waited for the next guy on Luke's team to go, then warily drew back his arrow, his arm visibly shaking even from her vantage point down the line. He sucked in his breath, and his first shot went over the target by a foot, disappearing into the golden field beyond.

He scowled, and Emma bunched the cuffs of her hoodie in her hands. Max used to have that same expression when pushed past his emotional limit. It was the same scowl she'd seen when his friend got sick in the backseat of his truck the day after he'd vacuumed it out for their first date. And the same scowl he wore when he saw Emma talking to a guy from her church youth group at the grocery store about a week later.

Did he recognize the expression at all? Would anyone else notice the similarities? Their matching cowlicks, identical eyes…

Max broke apart from the team and approached Cody, and her heart squeezed. He bent slightly to talk to him privately, clearly instructing him on how to better grasp the bow. He demonstrated, and Cody mimicked the motion with concentration.

The could-have-beens and should-have-beens paraded through her mind in sickeningly slow motion. Max and Cody batting a whiffle ball. Max and Cody teetering on a two-wheel bike without training wheels. Max and Cody in grease-stained jeans, bent over the hood of his truck.

He'd missed all those opportunities to be a dad.

And Cody had missed all those opportunities to experience a father.

Emma tore her gaze away from them as Max jogged aside, allowing Cody space to prepare for his next shot. Cody raised the bow with a much steadier arm and frowned downwind as he focused on the target. Jarvis whispered something and nudged the guy next to him, and Emma chalked it up to the Lord's grace in Jarvis's favor that she didn't catch what it was.

Cody continued to hold his position, the lines of his face more determined than she'd ever seen. Her heart stammered, and she desperately wanted to pray. For him to hit the target. For him to find what he was so desperately seeking. For him to get through this entire experience in one piece.

For him and Max both to forgive her once they knew the truth.

She held her breath as Cody's amateur grip released. Her hopes soared along with the arrow as it shot straight and true in a steady arch toward the bull's-eye.

And landed just short of the target.

Chapter Thirteen

"You are allowed to take breaks, you know." Max put down his pen and studied her over the rim of his reading glasses, the likes of which Emma still couldn't get used to. The small black frames alluded more to college professor than cowboy, but the contradiction only added to Max's appeal. He made any look seem attractive.

Unfortunately, she was supposed to be concentrating on brainstorming new group projects with him—not admiring the way his hair curled slightly at his neck or the way his button-down work shirt strained slightly at the buttons, as if his broad chest couldn't be fully contained.

Definitely not.

"I'm on a break now." She straightened from her spot on the tan suede sofa, resisting the urge to stretch despite the kink in her neck. They'd agreed—reluctantly on her part—to work together in the living area of the main house while the kids enjoyed their recreation time. They were nearby if the other counselors needed them but were still situated privately enough to discuss upcoming events without overeager young ears.

And without being *too* private.

She fought a blush, hoping he couldn't read her thoughts as easily as he used to. "Faith is with the girls."

"I know where she is." Max grinned, and she quickly looked back at her notebook, which sadly held very few usable ideas. She just couldn't concentrate with Max so painfully close. Not after finally admitting to herself what his proximity did to her, even this many years later. But after all they'd experienced and shared together, how could she be immune?

If she could concoct an ex-boyfriend antidote, she'd be a billionaire.

"I just meant you're still working right now, helping me out like this, even if it's not directly with the kids. Whenever Faith relieves you, it's totally fine for you to go have some alone time, or visit your mom, or whatever you want." Max leaned forward from his position in the recliner across from her and reached for his canned soda on the end table. "I know this job can be exhausting. I just don't want you to feel trapped." He winced. "Especially since you're not getting paid."

Good thing she wasn't, or she'd have to refund every penny at the rate she was going. Maybe she'd covered some ground with Tonya originally, but she still hadn't been able to confirm anything one way or another, despite days of surveillance.

As for her progress with Stacy, well, Emma didn't know if anyone was capable of breaking down that stony exterior. At least she had Katie, who continued to be a bright spot in the camp.

"I'm not trapped." The words felt like a lie leaving her mouth, and she drummed her pen against the notepad in her lap. She was, in so many ways. But that wasn't really Max's fault. "I mean, I know I *can* leave. I just don't—" She caught herself before admitting she didn't want to visit her mom. She cleared her throat. "I prefer to stay."

The momentary smolder in Max's eyes hinted at his seconding that particular choice, and she blinked quickly to bat it away. Glimpses of the old Max, the one she fell for so many years ago, kept sporadically popping to the surface, catching her heart unaware. Just when she felt her guard was firmly in place, he'd make an inside joke from back in the day or shoot her that wink that had once left her breathless, and just like that, her armor chinked. "Besides, you needed my help with this."

Unless it was just an excuse to spend more time with her. She wouldn't put it past him—the old Max had been incredibly crafty and manipulative when he wanted to be. Had that personality trait gone by the wayside when he'd cleaned himself up? How much personality went away when one made such dramatic life changes, anyway? Or did God just tweak it to be used for good instead of bad?

Good questions. Too bad God didn't seem prone to give her direct answers anymore. She'd severed that connection with Him years ago, when she chose sin over what was right. When she succumbed to the same temptations she once judged in her peers.

When she was left to pay for the consequences all by herself.

Loud laughter suddenly rang out from the rec room down the hall, and warmth spread across Max's expression. "That's always nice to hear."

"Yeah. Unless they're laughing *at* someone." Her stomach clenched, remembering the way Jarvis had teased Cody during the archery competition the afternoon before. It still riled her inside, and worst of all, made her feel helpless.

She could handle fear. Rejection. Abandonment. Anger. Insecurity. Bring it on.

But helplessness? Her least favorite. She wanted to *act*. Fix. Be. Do. And at Camp Hope, she might as well be watching from behind a two-way mirror. All visual, zero interaction.

Helpless.

Again.

Max frowned as he set his soda can back on the table. "They don't pick on Cody 24/7, despite how it might look to you."

"Jarvis has pulled some kind of stunt with him

every time we're in the group projects." Emma wanted to draw a big line through the list of ideas she'd come up with on her page. If the group projects were what made the camp harder for her son, she'd rather just eliminate the whole thing.

"He's acting out for the girls. It happens like that at every camp."

Emma frowned. Max almost looked more amused than concerned. And there was nothing funny about it. "I don't think it's that simple. Something tells me Jarvis is more hard-core than that."

"Jarvis will realize it's a wasted effort soon enough, trust me."

He wasn't listening. "Sure. And meanwhile, my son is sacrificed."

Max arched an eyebrow at her. "Not fair."

He was right. It wasn't. She drew a deep breath and tightened her grip on her pen. She was lashing out because she had no control. Over Cody—or even her own heart. She might have seen warning signs in the past over guys like Jarvis, but Max probably had, too. And he was in charge of this one, not her.

"You're right." She glanced down at her notes, the words swimming as her vision blurred. "So, what about incorporating art into the kids' schedule?" She fought to keep her tone level and free of emotion. "For expression."

Max's mouth opened and shut twice, as if debating whether or not to push their previous topic, but he finally nodded. "Sounds good. Some of the teens would probably think it a chore, but I bet several would enjoy it. Could be helpful."

"And interesting, to see what they'd paint if they had complete freedom."

"Good idea." His eyes lit at the possibilities. "Maybe it'll open some doors into their subconscious for us." Before she could argue, he got up and joined her on the sofa, forcing her to scoot sideways several inches to avoid being sat on. "I'll set that up for tomorrow. It'll be a good Saturday project." He looked down at her notes, tilting his head sideways to read. "What else you got there?"

As much as it meant to her that he valued her opinion, she almost covered her list with her hand from embarrassment. At least she had scratched out where she'd accidentally doodled his name earlier. "Nothing much."

"Trust exercises?" Max pointed to an entry halfway down her sheet, under where she had drawn a line through *relay races*. "What do you mean by that?"

"You know, all the cliché, old-fashioned stuff they used to make us do at church youth camp."

He stilled, and she hesitated, not sure if she'd offended or just brought up a bad memory. She'd forgotten—Max hadn't gone to youth camps. He didn't grow up in the church with her—or any church, for that matter. "I don't know, actually."

She sidestepped the conversational pothole she'd

created and rushed forward. "Where you pair off into teams of two and take turns leading each other verbally through an obstacle course. Or falling backward on a short stool or chair to be caught by your partner." She'd always hated that one. Guess she had trust issues from way back.

He nodded, but his guarded gaze kept her from determining if he'd let go of whatever negative emotion had momentarily stirred. "I like that. Let's add that to the schedule, too." He met her eyes, and slowly the wall evaporated into a sincere smile. "You're good at this."

"I have a degree in this." She shrugged.

"No, it's a gift. Really." He reached over and brushed her hair off her shoulder. Her body stiffened on instinct, and she tried to relax to keep from letting him know how much it affected her. "You're a natural."

Then why was Cody still immune? Why was Tonya shutting her out from her problems? Why did Stacy attempt to shoot daggers with her eyes? She should say "thank you" to be polite, but she wouldn't mean it. Couldn't sincerely accept the compliment. So she stayed silent, wondering what she'd do if Max touched her again.

Wondering what she'd do if he didn't.

The heater kicked on, and the gentle whirring noise blended with the sound of the kids interacting down the hall. She edged a few more inches away, under the pretense of closing up her notes.

"Let me know if you need help getting the art supplies. I could run into town tonight or in the morning for the paint and brushes. We'll need canvases, too, and easels, unless you just want to—"

"What happened with Cody's father?"

Her stomach constricted like she'd been punched. She sucked in air, but it didn't refresh. Rather, it stuck in her nose, her throat, choked her. She coughed, lungs aching. Or maybe that was her heart.

Max held up both hands. "I know that was left field. But I've been wondering for a while now, and well…I didn't know if that was a sore subject or not. I'm sorry."

He didn't sound very sorry. She inhaled again, and this time, the oxygen revived. Her blood pulsed through her veins, and she twisted to face Max on the couch, pulling one of her legs up between them. If she could have this conversation from across the room without raising more suspicion, she'd try it.

That is, if her dramatic reaction hadn't already given her away.

"Sore subject?" She echoed, unable to say more. If he only knew. But no, he couldn't know, because of the typo. She pulled in her lower lip. Could Max hear her runaway heartbeat? How could she lie to him flat out? Maybe she'd been doing that for years, but doing so from a distance felt a whole lot different. Maybe she hadn't been responsible for that typo, but she hadn't corrected it, either. "It's not a great one."

"I've been trying to talk to Cody about it." Max shrugged, looking pained. Maybe the conversation was more awkward for him than she thought. Especially if Max's feelings for her were as strong as Rachel had let on. Did he assume she'd married, or kept up her less than pure ways as she'd had with him? But he'd been her only.

"He's pretty shut down," Max continued, rubbing at a callous on his palm. "I've hit a wall, and I thought any information you could share would help."

She fought back a sarcastic snort and turned it into a cough. Oh, the irony. "There's not much to say." Much she *could* say, was more like it.

"So I take it Cody has never met his dad?"

He was twisting the knife and didn't have a clue. She pressed her hand to her chest, the pressure of his words as tangible as a weapon. How could she answer without lying?

He must have taken her silence for a confirmation. "Is that your choice?" Max frowned, clearly confused. "Or the father's?"

Tears sprung, and she fought to keep them below the surface. "All of those, I guess." Not true, though. The real father had had zero choice in the matter, but the choices he *did* make had left Emma with none. She clenched her hand into a fist. Such a complicated, confusing cycle.

"I don't know your situation. But I know a boy's relationship with his dad is crucial, and that void—"

"No!" Emma leaped off the couch, unable to sit that close another second with her secret weighing so heavily. She stared down at Max's stricken expression, feeling her heart crumble into dust at her feet and helpless to stop it. "Just drop it, okay?"

His features morphed into a careful, practiced mask. One she knew from experience—she donned the same one when dealing with irate clients in her office. "Look, if it's a bad situation, I understand. But anything you can tell me about this guy—"

"There's nothing you need to know about him." She had to stop this conversation now. What if she accidentally said "you" instead of "him"? The pressure building inside her head threatened to explode. She jabbed her fingers into her temples and briefly closed her eyes. "Just trust me on this. It's for Cody's own good." Not that he had any more reason to trust her than she did him.

Max rose and stood before her, reaching for her hands. She jerked them away, avoiding the hurt in his eyes. "Emma. Talk to me."

No. If she said anything else, she'd say too much. Especially with the tenderness in his voice, the compassion in his gaze. The sincerity in his touch.

Time to leave.

"I'll be back in a bit." She grabbed her notebook from the couch, stuck the pen behind her ear and marched to the kitchen door before she—or he—

could change her mind. "I'm taking that break you mentioned."

Visiting her mom had never seemed so appealing.

Max stared out the window into the afternoon sun as Emma bolted to her car, spraying gravel in an exit worthy of a Golden Globe nod. How did they go from having a comfortably quiet time together, to a really productive talk about the campers, to Emma running out nearly in tears from the room? From the entire ranch, for that matter?

Cody's father must have hurt her worse than he'd imagined.

He probably looked like a real winner, too, dredging it all up. Still, he needed to know the basics, for Cody's sake.

And maybe a little for his own sake.

Max slapped his notebook closed and began gathering the pens and highlighters they'd used. Emma had chosen pink, of course. She'd always loved pink. The one time he'd brought her flowers—okay, they'd been stolen from a neighbor's rosebush, and still had the thorns, but it still counted—he'd made sure to find pink ones. And not that pale, flimsy pink, either, that seemed like it'd fade before it could be appreciated. Emma needed bright pink. A statement color.

The kind that stained and lingered.

He headed for his office to put away their notes

and almost ran into Mama Jeanie, who was coming out of the kitchen, drying her hands on a dish towel.

"Land sakes, boy! You trying to give an old woman a heart attack?" She planted both fists on her apron-clad hips and grinned to take the sting out. "Then who would cook supper for all those kids of yours?"

"The pizza joint in town." He grinned back, grateful for the break from the heaviness that'd taken over the minute he'd popped the father question to Emma. He should have known better. But if he didn't ask, how could he find out? It was hardly something to look up on Google.

Mama Jeanie's wrinkled but wise face slowly drifted into a frown. "I saw that new counselor, Miss Emma, tearing out of here like a rabbit from a fox." Her dark brows wrinkled deeper as she peered up at him with expectation. "What did the fox say?"

If anyone else had insinuated such a thing, he'd have been offended, and probably smarted off. But not to Mama Jeanie. Never to Mama Jeanie. He licked his lips, then shrugged. "Was something personal, apparently." To put it mildly. He wondered if she saw through his attraction to Emma. The woman missed nothing. At least she stuck to the kitchen, because if she ever found that picture he'd kept of Emma and him all these years…

"If it was personal, then why were you nosing around in it?" She inched toward him, and despite the fact that she had to be almost six inches shorter, Max felt like backing up a step.

He resisted the urge and placed a friendly hand on Mama Jeanie's shoulder. "I'm just doing my job." He tried to step around her to his office, but she sidestepped with the spryness of someone half her age.

"I do more around this camp than just cook, you know." She crossed her arms, the dish towel dangling from two bony but capable fingers. "I observe. I listen. And I hear."

"You just said that."

"Uh-huh." She waved her finger at him and grinned, her teeth stark white against her brown complexion. "Hearing and listening are not the same." She leaned closer, and this time, he backed up. "You should try more of the latter."

Well that was cryptic.

"Anyway." She waved the towel like a white flag. "Turkey and dressing all right for the Thanksgiving dinner?"

He blinked in an effort to keep up, feeling as winded as if he'd just run a 10k. "Thanksgiving dinner?"

"Remember? Before this session started, you said it'd be nice to have a Thanksgiving feast the last week of camp. Before the real holiday began."

Oh, yeah, he had said that—especially considering several of these kids came from home situations where they might not have a traditional meal. He nodded, grateful for the subject change. "Yes, that sounds perfect. With all the usual trimmings. If we need more for the grocery budget, let me know. I'll call the church."

Broken Bend Church of Grace was their biggest supporter, along with several other wealthier families in the county. He'd get whatever donations were needed—when it came to the campers, he learned a long time ago to choke off any lingering traces of his self-pride. The kids were worth it.

"I've cooked on a shoestring budget for years, my boy. I'm not afraid of the challenge now." She snapped the towel good-naturedly at him before heading back to her kitchen haven.

Max took the opportunity to dart inside his office and shut the door. He dumped the office supplies he'd been holding onto his desk and slumped against the corner of it. The wood dug into the leg of his jeans, but he didn't move. Mama Jeanie's words kept playing in his head, a strange echo to Emma's reaction to his question.

It all meant something. But what? What wasn't he hearing?

Emma's voice sounded next, as clear and vivid in his memories as the night he first told her he loved her. That had led to a more physical expression, but the words themselves—for the first time in his life—hadn't been spoken for that reason. No, he'd meant them.

And hadn't stopped meaning them yet.

There's nothing you need to know about him. It's for Cody's own good.

The panic behind her short sentences hinted at more to the story. Did that mean even Emma didn't know who Cody's father was? That thought left a bitter taste in his mouth. No way. Not Emma. Or was she a victim? But if she'd been attacked, why the secrecy?

Nothing made sense.

God, some wisdom. Discernment. Something, please. He bowed his head and prayed, but the words felt as if they didn't filter past the roof. And then he was struck with the certainty that it didn't matter. Whatever Emma had gone through or however she had lived in the years since they'd parted ways, it didn't really matter.

It didn't change his past or current feelings for her one iota. After all, whose past was squeaky clean? His was dirty enough to make even an infomercial cleaner give up. At least God hadn't given up on him. That was enough.

And that was why he needed to pay it forward. Whatever it took, he would make sure Emma knew that she was still worthwhile. A treasure. Priceless. To him, and to God.

And even to her son.

Chapter Fourteen

Her mom knelt in the small garden to the left of the house, digging in the dirt with the same stained, floral-print gloves she'd worn when Emma was a child. Those gloves, with the tiny rosebuds once red and now faded pink, had been a fixture in the house for as long as Emma could remember. Lying on the counter by the sink where she'd washed her hands after gardening. Lying on the floor by her Bible in the living room, where she'd shucked them before having her evening quiet time. Lying on the porch swing where she'd taken her last tea break.

Emma watched her work for a moment, allowing the warmth of the sun on her shoulders to ease the chill of her conversation with Max. She'd almost bought her mother a new pair of gloves during her last Christmas at home, back before she left for college. Back before her father died. Back before she'd gotten involved with Max and changed her entire course of life.

Maybe familiar wasn't always so bad, after all.

She shoved her keys in her pocket and crossed the front yard to stand behind her mother.

"Emma?" Mom turned with a slight smile—or was it a grimace—and lifted one hand to shade her eyes from the late-afternoon sun. "What are you doing here?"

The question was innocent enough, as was the tone accompanying it, but it still dug in like a burr. She fought off a wave of frustration. Couldn't she just be visiting her mother while in town? Why did she need an explanation? She drew a deep breath, trying to convince herself it wasn't that bad, that her defenses were just up because of Max's probing.

But it felt like more than that. Her mom had never treated her the same way after she'd gotten pregnant.

Or maybe she'd never treated her mom the same way after.

"Just taking a break." She folded her arms against her chest, then recognized the vibe the body language gave and forced herself to lower her hands to her sides. "Max said I could."

No idea why she added that last part. As if she needed Max Ringgold's permission for anything. He'd been the reason she'd wound up where she was—and Cody, too. She hadn't asked Max for permission or help thirteen years ago, and the thought of starting now made the indignant, self-sufficient woman inside her cringe in her high-heeled career shoes.

And made the counselor inside her realize just how many issues she still had with various factors of Broken Bend.

Her mom rocked back, eyes narrowed, except this time it wasn't because of the sunshine. Guess Emma's intuition and knack for probing into others lives came from somewhere honest. "Let's go have tea."

"No, Mom. You're gardening." She wasn't about to interrupt her mother's routine, or she'd never hear the end of it—whether from her family or herself. Besides, despite Mom's strong belief, tea *didn't* cure everything. She dropped to her knees in the grass instead and gestured toward the rows of seeds. "Carry on."

Mom adjusted one of her gloves, hesitated with another sharp glance and then obeyed, continuing to pluck weeds from the stubborn patch of earth surrounding her meticulous lines of soon-to-be-vegetables.

Emma tentatively reached for another section of weeds, in spite of her lack of gloves, and tore the skinny green intruders from the earth. She hated to sit and do nothing, and maybe if she worked, they wouldn't talk as much.

No such luck.

"How's Cody?"

Wasn't that the question of the hour? She

schooled her expression into an indifferent mask, not willing to let her mom know just how much was riding on the next couple weeks. "He's as good as he can be. Making progress."

Mom nodded as she shifted over to the next row, the pile of discarded weeds beside her growing taller as she worked. "And the girls you're counseling?"

Why was everyone shooting questions from the hip today? "Doing okay." She ripped out another, surprised at the level of stress relief the simple action brought. She might not be able to make a difference where it counted, but she could make a difference to this garden. In both appearance and substance.

"So everyone is okay."

Her mom's tone hinted at her disbelief, and Emma couldn't blame her. But that didn't mean she wanted to open the floodgates of confession, either. Because once the words—and the tears—started, they might not stop.

"It's a good thing you're there, then."

Emma sat back and stretched her shoulders, bracing herself for something else hard to hear. "Why's that?"

Her mother continued working as if the tension between them didn't exist. And for her, maybe it didn't. She'd always leaned toward being oblivious. "You have a gift for making 'okay' turn out better than okay."

A compliment. From her mother. And it wasn't even Christmas.

Emma stared at the tiny rows of seeds, eagerly waiting to sprout. They had no idea the danger they'd been in from the weeds, no idea the death they'd be sure to experience had the gardener not come and tended them.

Just like Cody had yet to fully grasp the ramifications of his actions. Like Max had no idea the bomb she would eventually drop on his carefully reformed world.

Oblivious. Like she'd been before trading her innocence for a short-lived ride with rebellion. And all for the sake of what? Proving a point? Testing her limits? Escaping the supersticky label of "Good Girl"? All she'd done is trade it for another label she couldn't tear off.

Tears pricked her eyes, and her chest tightened. The floral print on her mom's gloves blurred into a pastel jumble. Suddenly, she wasn't a grown woman anymore with a successful practice in a big city. She was eighteen again, and scared, and alone—and overcome with feelings she couldn't identify or ignore.

Before she could stop herself, she reached out and grabbed her mother's arm.

Mom immediately stopped and turned, covering Emma's bare hand with her dirty gloved one, and raised her eyebrows without speaking. The acceptance in her gaze was nearly Emma's undoing, and she blurted out the truth for the first time in thirteen years.

"Max is Cody's father."

Max wasn't sure if the art expression project Emma created had been pure genius or pure torture.

He squinted at the rows of easels before him, set up in the early-morning sunshine near the barn. They didn't have an indoor spot in the camp big enough to house all the campers and easels at one time that wouldn't suffer from paint splatters, so Luke and Tim spread some tarp on the grass, lined up folding chairs and let them go.

Max paced absently behind the rows of folding chairs, hanging back to give the teens room to create while keeping an eye out for Emma. He hadn't seen her return to Camp Hope yesterday, though he'd kept a subtle watch for her. She'd shown up at dinner as expected last night, though, relieving Faith to go home to her family. But after dinner, she'd taken the girls on to their next activity without giving him more than a passing nod. Breakfast had gone pretty much the same way.

He didn't know exactly how to smooth things over between them, but ignoring it didn't seem the best way to go. He wasn't sure which was worse—her avoiding him, or the awkward tension that hovered when they had to be in the same room. How was he going to meet his new goal if she refused to speak to him? Somehow, he had to show her he was legit. That she could trust him. Maybe she was right not to when they were younger. He hadn't been ready for a heart like hers.

But now...

He wanted the chance to earn it back. To show her that nothing was lost forever. That she and Cody would find their way out of this, with God at their side—and hopefully with him right there, too.

"That's beautiful, Katie."

Emma's sudden voice to his left both warmed him and created shivers on the back of his neck, all at once. Max drew a deep breath to resist rushing to her side and slowly adjusted his cowboy hat so he wouldn't do something stupid—like sweep her in his arms.

Emma stood behind Katie's easel, where the perky redhead sat with paintbrush poised, sweatshirt sleeves pushed up to her elbows. She'd painted the barn beside them, complete with rolling golden hills of pasture. A dark blob on the farthest hilltop hinted at a horse. Or maybe a cow.

Max squinted. Maybe a rhino.

"I love the barn. Nice detail."

Katie beamed under Emma's praise, and Max had the sudden urge to earn her compliments, as well. He joined them, hesitantly, as one would approach a startled stallion. "Emma's right. Very nice job." With the exception of the unidentified hilltop creature, but hey. They weren't giving lessons here. They were letting the kids express themselves. Speaking of…he had the perfect excuse to talk to Emma.

Alone.

"Join me?" He touched her elbow, trying to ignore the hurt that radiated when she stiffened in response, and led her several yards away where they could talk quietly without being overheard. "What do you think so far?"

Panic laced her eyes before her gaze settled on the easels. "You mean about the paintings."

"What else would I mean—" Max cut himself off. "Emma. Are we going to ignore the elephant here or go ahead and take care of him one bite at a time?"

A tiny smile teased the corners of her lips. Man, she was beautiful. "I think you're mixing metaphors." A spark lit her eyes and ignited his stomach with memories.

"Some things never change." He grinned. "Remember when I meant to say pretty as a picture, and I said pretty as a catcher?" He'd had a few in him at the time, but he clearly remembered the confused expression on Emma's face as they sat on the tailgate of his truck, stargazing. And the embarrassment that had flooded afterward. At least she'd thought his blunder was cute.

Or he'd thought she thought so.

Emma snorted, shoulder bumping him like old

times. "You do realize by now that it's *picture,* not *pitcher?*"

"Come on, now. I'm not that hopeless."

Her eyes met his and held for a moment before she directed her attention back to the teens.

Oops. Now what? The sadness in her expression nearly stole his breath. "What is it?" Did she still believe him that far gone, even after all he'd done in her absence? After all he'd cleaned up and changed and accomplished?

A light breeze brushed strands of hair over her eyes, blocking his view of her stoic profile. She didn't reach up to brush them back, so he did.

"Just...thinking." She fluttered her hand to wave off the topic, as though it was as easily shooed as a summer bee. At least she didn't dodge his touch this time.

He turned so he faced her, giving her his full attention. She deserved nothing less. "Elephant, remember? Here's a fork."

"That's seriously gross." But the smile was back, and the sadness slightly dissipated. Mission accomplished—even if she still kept her profile to him. Then she sobered. "You're not hopeless, Max."

Well, at least there was that. "You do realize the same is true for you?" He wanted to touch her again but knew she'd spook. Not to mention they stood behind ten teenagers all eager for gossip and rumors—including Emma's own son.

"I know."

But did she really? Her lips pressed together in a thin line, and she wrapped her arms around herself, rubbing her forearms with her hands. He started to shrug out of his zip-up hoodie, but she shook her head to stop him. "It wouldn't look right."

"What? Teaching these guys how to act like a gentleman?" But he zipped it back up at the stubborn glint in her eye. Time to change the subject before he pushed her any farther into a corner. He'd gotten two smiles out of her and broken the iceberg that had risen between them last night. That'd have to be enough for now. "So, what do you think?" He gestured to the easels.

This time she launched right into her opinions, saving them from any more painful banter. "Katie's painting is detailed, like you said, which I feel lends to her personality. She likes things neat, together and orderly. But it's also bright and happy—how she feels right now. She's in a good place."

He nodded, absorbing the picture. Maybe too good a place. Was anyone that happy at a camp for troubled teens? It wasn't like they were here for s'mores and Monopoly. He still felt as if something was missing from Katie's file, but he couldn't read information that wasn't there. Maybe he was just paranoid.

"What about Stacy's?" The abstract swirls of blues, greens and purples sort of lent to a teenaged version of van Gogh's *Starry Night*—Max's favorite painting for its cryptic beauty. He hoped Emma picked up a good impression from it, too. He worried about Stacy. Of all his students, she'd been the most blocked in their One4One talks.

"To me, it looks like twilight. And I think those splotches at the top are supposed to represent stars." She tilted her head to get a better view. "But the important part to realize about hers is the color choice. The blue color family represents peace, relaxation and tranquility. That hints at how she's not nearly as hardened inside as she appears on the outside. There's a wall up, for sure—but the foundation of it doesn't go deep." She hesitated. "Maybe one of us will reach her."

"If anyone can, it's you."

Emma winced at the compliment, as if she didn't fully believe it, but he didn't care. He'd keep sprinkling the truth on her until her confidence grew. He'd seen her with the girls and knew what she had already accomplished with them. She might not see it, but he did. So did God. Nothing was being wasted, however small it might seem on the surface.

Hopefully that same principle would remain true as he pursued her.

He wanted to ask about Cody's painting next but didn't dare. Then Emma's gaze lingered on it, and he knew from her quick intake of breath the diagnosis wasn't as favorable as the others. The painting in front of the boy contained a careful red circle that took up nearly the entire canvas. A thick black slant slashed across the center of the circle diagonally, the universal symbol for *no*.

Max frowned. No…no what?

One glance at Emma's crestfallen expression determined she wasn't sure, either. No to Camp Hope? No to authority? No to rules? Or was it a more positive portrayal, as in, no more fighting? No more crimes? No more misbehaving?

He couldn't be sure. But he didn't need a course in symbolism to conclude that the dripping red and black paint spoke of intense feelings, likely anger. Maybe even hatred. Cody was dealing with something hard-core, and until their next One4One chat, he wouldn't get a chance to find out. He couldn't exactly march over and demand an explanation. The last thing they needed was to judge the kids based on their project. This was supposed to be a safe exercise, a chance for them to express themselves, though he did caution them ahead of time about keeping the paintings PG—no nudity or curse words, or they'd lose recreation time for a week.

"What about Tonya's?" He couldn't see the girl's entire canvas from here, but it had to be more encouraging than Cody's—and right now, the best gift he could give Emma was distraction as well as prompting her to use her training productively.

He hated the helpless gleam in her eye and sent up a quick prayer that God would redeem their situation ASAP. Something would give, soon.

It had to.

Emma straightened her shoulders, and he wanted to applaud the way she gathered herself together, despite the trauma still lingering in her eyes as she focused on Tonya's project. "I'm not sure. I can't tell."

They both eased sideways several paces until they could see around her bent head, still hunched over her painting as she did detail work at the bottom. The top of Tonya's easel was covered in pastel stripes, representing a sunset or sunrise.

"I still can't see the rest. It looks like a self-portrait, maybe? Those look like her black braids." Emma craned her neck as she spoke.

Max did the same. The painting held promise, what he could see of it—much less amateur in style than the others. Tonya was either a natural or had taken classes at some point. The eyes on the figure she was painting appeared nearly alive, while the cheery background hinted at a lighthearted mood that well complemented the young girl in the drawing.

Then Tonya leaned back, paintbrush lowering, and studied the portrait, allowing Max and Emma a full view—of a beautiful, African-American girl with braids, vivid eyes...

And a distorted, wide-open jaw that yawned and swirled off her face.

He shot a startled glance at Emma, whose eyes widened in recognition. When she finally spoke, it was to confirm what Max already knew.

"Tonya has a secret."

Chapter Fifteen

Emma never thought she'd ever seek solace in a dusty barn stall, but the repetitive motion of running a currycomb through Remington's mane somehow brought as much relaxation as her last spa trip.

Maybe more.

Remington shifted his weight, bobbing his head slightly and leaning into her smooth stroking. Maybe the extra attention was just what the horse needed, too.

Emma slowed as she worked through a tangle. Tonya's painting from yesterday weighed heavily on her spirit, almost as much as Cody's did. She whispered to Remington. "Did Tonya tell you her secrets before she fainted?"

Remington's ears flicked forward at her voice, and then he snorted through his nose.

She kept brushing, trying not to dwell on the fact

she had just resorted to talking to animals. "I understand. Confidences are confidences."

Sort of like how it seemed evident Stacy knew something about Tonya that she wasn't telling. Did the older girl know Tonya had been faking her illness the other day and was holding it over her? It seemed a valid possibility, but Emma couldn't reconcile with the idea that Tonya would care so strongly about pretending to be sick. It'd be easier to just admit the truth now and take the consequence than cater to Stacy's whims.

Or would it? Emma sure wasn't taking that advice herself.

She pushed the uncomfortable thought aside, finishing the tangle before moving to the next portion of mane, the dark strands wiry between her fingers. The girls were finishing up breakfast, and she'd excused herself to start chores early and have a minute to de-stress—before the constant chatter, brooding and occasional whining from her charges began. Even after the optional Bible study that morning before breakfast, they seemed grumpy, as though they sensed something in the air. Maybe because only half the kids had attended the study.

She felt disgruntled herself. Sitting across from Max and listening to him read the Bible for fifteen minutes left her breakfast lodged in her stomach like a rock, heaping guilt in generous dollops on top.

And her mother...Emma paused, her fingers

knotted in Remington's mane. Her garden-side revelation had brought more regret than relief, though it was sort of freeing to know a living soul finally knew her dirty little secret.

Slowly, she unclenched the strands of horse hair and resumed her brushing, stomach knotting instead. Her mom had taken the news a little better than Emma had suspected. But her words lingered.

Broken Bend's bad boy transitioned into a solid, God-fearing man, Emma. If you'd told me the truth from the beginning, I could have let you know that.

After Emma's immediate defense, which went over her mom's head as usual, more words left a permanent mark.

It could have been different, Emma. So much different. For all of you.

The weight of those words latched on to her shoulders and clung for dear life. She might as well name the baggage she'd just acquired, because it wasn't going anywhere.

Her mother was right in one regard. But in another, she still didn't understand. No one did. And unless they had been pregnant, rejected and alone, watching the man who promised that his love for her transcended any addiction live out his lie in neon color, well—they never would.

Besides, who was to say that it wasn't intentional? If she'd stuck around that day she caught Max in the middle of a deal, would he still have eventually changed and devoted his life to helping others? Or would she somehow have derailed God's plan even further?

Regardless, whatever Max had become didn't change what he'd been.

She dropped the brush in the grooming bucket she'd snagged from the tack room and rubbed Remington's neck. "Don't count on this behavior from me regularly." Weird that she wasn't already craving a hot stone massage treatment by now, one of her more frequent rewards for her stressful career in Dallas. Maybe there was something to be said for open skies and fresh air, after all.

Now, if only it'd work on Cody.

Remington snuffled the hand she held in front of his nose, and she grimaced at the soft, wet horse skin. "It'll take more than that to convince me, you know."

"Convince you of what?" Max appeared in front of the stall door, and Emma jumped. A petite blonde stood beside him, wearing a T-shirt with the fire department logo blazoned across the front.

Emma stepped away from Remington, his head bobbing at her abrupt movements. "Nothing." She tried to smile and pretend like she wasn't caught talking to a horse, though with Max's lifestyle now he probably wouldn't have thought twice. But who was his friend, and what would she think? "Just waiting on the girls to get here."

"You might want to go check on them." Max frowned, glancing at his watch. "Breakfast was cleared away fifteen minutes ago, and they're supposed to come straight out here for chores."

"Maybe they needed a bathroom break." Emma started to open the stall door, and Max stepped back to give her room.

"This is Caley, by the way. Brady's wife."

Caley held out her hand, her grip warm and solid. "Nice to meet you. I've—" She swallowed the rest of her sentence and finished with a smile, instead. But the unspoken words lingered. *I've heard a lot about you.*

Emma still wasn't sure how they made her feel, but the dividing line teetered more toward good than bad, and she wasn't sure how she felt about that, either.

Time to go. "Thanks. I better go check on the girls." Max was probably being paranoid, considering how long girls took prepping in the bathroom and knowing how they did anything possible to legitimately stall their chores, but at least this way she wouldn't have to make awkward small talk with Caley. If Brady knew about her, then it went without saying Caley did, too.

Max's voice followed her down the barn aisle. "Caley's here to meet the girls, so why doesn't she go with you?"

She paused and turned slowly. "Sure." Talk about awkward. Hopefully Caley wouldn't want to talk about her and Max. Or anything to do with Max, for that matter. Not while her heart still tottered on her sleeve, her secret one breath away from being revealed.

Caley fell into step beside Emma as they made their way to the dorm. "Max wanted me to come speak to the girls at some point before camp was over, sort of show them what it looked like to follow a career dream." She lifted one slim shoulder in a shrug. "I'm a firefighter, and he thinks they could use encouragement, since most of his campers don't have good home lives. Sort of like I'm proof they can succeed even when they feel the odds are stacked against them."

Her defense against Caley dissolved slightly. "That's not a bad idea." Wow, Max thought of everything. He seemed truly invested in each of his campers lives, especially to go to such effort to cover every element of their future.

Caley's eyes shone. "I'm happy to help. I've been through some stuff in the past, and while it's probably nothing like these girls, we're all in need of grace."

Wasn't that the truth. Her steps faltered. She knew God gave grace to sinners…but what about when those sinners knew better, like she did when she messed up by getting involved emotionally and then physically with Max? Did that cancel it out? Or did she just have to pay more consequences, like now, with Cody's rebellion and her own struggle regarding her feelings for his dad?

Thankfully they reached the dorms before she could determine an answer—if there even was one.

Emma stepped inside the temporary building. "Girls? There's someone here to meet you. And by the way, you're late for chores."

Katie and Stacy looked up with guilt-ridden expressions as they hunched on the side of Tonya's bed, whispering furtively. Tonya was nowhere to be seen.

Emma stopped and crossed her arms. "Okay, that's it. What do you know?"

Katie looked away, and Stacy smirked as if confident she knew Emma couldn't force her to tell. "Well, let's see. Two plus two equals four, and the capital of Louisiana is—"

Caley snorted beside her, and covered it with a cough.

It would have been funny to Emma, too, though still disrespectful—but Caley didn't know the whole story about Tonya, and there was nothing funny right now about the fact the girl wasn't in her room, and her roommates were sharing secrets. Secrets Emma needed to know.

"To the barn. Now. Caley will walk you." Let the firefighter introduce herself on the way. She caught the blonde's eye, and Caley immediately nodded and ushered the girls out the door. "Max has told me a lot about you" were her trailing words as the door closed behind them.

Well at least she got to say it to someone.

Emma paced the small walkway between the beds, wishing the quilts could talk. She needed to alert Max in case Tonya had run away, but first, she wanted to figure out what was going on. Why had the other girls landed on Tonya's bed to share secrets if she wasn't here? Probably implied Tonya had been there recently. Maybe she and Caley had missed her on their way from the barn. Maybe Tonya hadn't run away, just gotten upset and walked out first instead of coming over for chores together. Had the girls upset her?

She didn't want to overreact, but she really didn't want to under-react, either.

She stopped in front of the bathroom door, noticing the light on and the toilet running. Might be leaky, unless someone had just used it before she came in. She looked inside, unsure what she was searching for.

Her gaze caught on the trash can tucked between the toilet and the counter, and she sucked in her breath.

Remington and the bed quilts might not be giving Tonya's secrets up—but the wastebasket sure did.

Max stood back, surveying the rows of folding chairs spread across the sun-dried grass, splotches of red and blue paint evident on several patches where the tarps had failed. Trust exercises. He still wasn't sure about this, but Emma seemed to know what she was talking about, and he wanted to incorporate her ideas. Wanted her to feel as though she was a part of this.

He knew how terrible it felt to be involved in something up to your eyebrows and still have zero control. For him, it'd been a drug addiction. For Emma, it was watching her son spiral beneath her grasp.

With God's help, he'd beaten his. Hopefully he'd get to see Emma and Cody share a similar victory.

The kids' voices rose on the brisk November wind as the gang filed toward him, led by Chaplain Tim, past the makeshift obstacle course he'd thrown together and wearing dubious expressions he probably mirrored. He quickly schooled his features to hopefully resemble confidence. This would go well. How could it not?

"Another obstacle course? The other one looked harder." Cody's voice carried on the breeze and held two parts bravado, one part trepidation. He'd struggled on the rope swing of the first obstacle course, which had set him and Jarvis at each other—no wonder he'd be wary about this one, even if by all appearances it seemed a huge step down on the difficulty factor.

But the teens didn't know yet they'd be doing this one blindfolded.

"It was only hard for you." Jarvis snorted under his breath as he drew near, and Max shot him a warning look that wilted his arrogant expression.

No way was that getting started today. In fact… Max grinned as he glanced at the red bandanas waiting on one of the folding chairs.

He knew who Cody's partner would be.

Emma brought up the rear of the group with the girls, who Caley had brought to him in the barn earlier that morning. Stacy and Katie had acted a little odd, but he figured it was just for getting busted for lingering in the dorm after breakfast instead of coming out to do chores. Tonya had gone right to work, even volunteering to soap saddles, the one chore the girls especially hated because of getting the polish under their nails. Despite her eagerness, he'd still have to handle the girls' disobedience eventually, once he decided which punishment fit the crime. Maybe he'd ask Emma for her suggestions.

But in spite of his attempts to catch her eye, she remained fixated on the girls, as though afraid they'd disappear if she didn't stare directly at them. He frowned. Weird. Something was definitely going on, and judging by Emma's pale expression, he might have more discipline coming up than he'd thought.

Time for that later. Right now he had a horde of teens to blindfold and attempt to teach about trust.

"Line up." He motioned for the guys to take one line and the girls another, then realized the girls were unevenly numbered. Who would sit out? Unless Emma took a spot.

He made a quick decision. "Stacy and Katie, you're partners. Grab a blindfold. Emma and Tonya, you two will pair up." He raised his eyebrows at Emma, and after a quick wince, she nodded. He hated to put her through the paces with the teens, but the girls couldn't miss it and he had no reason to keep one of them out. They needed the experience.

"David and Ashton." He motioned for them to take their blindfolds. "Jarvis and Cody."

He heard Emma's gasp before her gaze landed on him, probably in an attempt to shoot some sort of fire. Well, maybe he deserved it, because it did seem mean on the surface. But he'd been doing this a long time, and Emma had to trust him.

Too bad she couldn't just fall off a chair, let him catch her and be done with it.

Jarvis's and Cody's protests mingled, but he waved them off and continued assigning partners. Grumbles permeated the group. Good, that must mean he was on the right track. What was the point in learning to trust someone you were already buddy-buddy with?

He let Stacy and Katie go first through the obstacle course, Stacy blindfolded, which she clearly hated, and Katie leading her, which she clearly loved. They managed to get through the maze of cones, chairs and low-slung ropes with only one or two banged knees. The guys went next, teasing each other and not taking it as seriously as Max hoped.

Until it was time to reverse, and the tormenter became the tormented.

"The golden rule exists for a reason, guys," Max hollered as snickers rose from revenge being played. Ashton crashed into a chair as David snorted in amusement. "Do unto others, and all that. Not so fun on the other side, is it?"

The lesson finally sank in as the boys began taking the course seriously, leading each other through unscathed. Finally. "Chairs are next."

More groans, along with quibbles over who would go first and on which team. "That'll be Tim's decision." Max shut down that argument quick. "Emma? A second?"

She joined him on the fringes of the group as Tim began lining up the teams in front of the row of chairs. "You okay with this? I know I put you on the spot."

"It's fine." Her eyes darted to Tonya, then back to his face, something guarded and downright strange in her gaze. "It's just…I found out…" Her voice trailed, and he wished they were alone so he could cup her chin and make her look at him.

"Found out what? Her secret?"

"It's not what you think." Emma glanced back at the girls before meeting his eyes briefly. "I can't tell you here." She pulled in her lower lip, looking nearly like a teen herself.

Not what he thought? Then what else was there—and why was it bothering Emma so deeply? He grazed her arm with his fingers, forgetting about their audience. "Are you all right?"

She jerked at his touch but didn't pull away. "We'll talk later. Let's do this."

She was more willing to fall backward off a chair than talk about Tonya, so it had to be bad. Or maybe it really was that private.

He led them back to the group, where Tim had gotten the first set of teams on the chairs and ready. This time, one person would fall while three caught them. They couldn't do their original teams of one on one, since there were several teams where one person significantly outweighed the other. He didn't want to send a whole crew to the E.R.

"Hands crossed across your chest, cupping each of your shoulders." Max pointed to Cody, who stood on the chair, for once looking vulnerable. Jarvis, David and Ashton gathered beneath him, arms outstretched. "When you're ready, trust— and fall backward."

Cody snorted in disbelief, and Tonya, who stood on the chair beside him in front of Emma, Stacy and Katie, looked as if she might faint again.

"When you're ready." Max waited. So did Cody and Tonya, not budging. The seconds on his watch ticked away, and the groups of teens with outstretched arms grew restless, shifting their weight and sighing.

"Okay, forget that. On three." He cleared his throat, a wariness of his own suddenly creeping into his stomach. Must be picking up the kids' nervousness. "One."

Cody coughed. The kids below him stretched their arms farther, gathered in tighter.

"Two."

Tonya sucked in her breath. Katie and Stacy squeezed in, Emma's eyes darting back and forth from Tonya to Cody as if she weren't sure who she'd rather catch.

"Three."

Tonya fell into the arms of her friends.

And Cody landed flat on his back in the dust.

Chapter Sixteen

"What a day." Max leaned against the wooden fence railing, propping one booted foot on the rail behind him. He yanked off his hat and rubbed his hair, the gesture familiar and comforting yet at the same time, unnerving. Moonlight against his profile highlighted his rugged features, which looked as weary as she felt.

"You can say that again." Emma tried not to let him see her watching, tried not to let him see her hanging by a rapidly fraying thread. Was that even possible to hide anymore? Voices from the past rose up in a suffocating mist. She squeezed her eyes closed as memories assaulted, some from a decade ago, some from that very afternoon, sounds and images mixing and twirling in a cyclone she couldn't escape. The comfort of snuggling in Max's embrace on her parents' swing. The hardness in his eyes the day he accepted that last delivery of drugs. The beeping of the monitors while she was in labor with Cody. The slamming doors of his rebellion. The thud as Cody landed flat on his back in the dirt.

Max's voice softened. "He's okay, Emma. I promise."

He'd probably uttered those same words thirty-seven times in the past three hours, even after she'd seen for herself Cody was fine and moved on to the next activity as planned. But the assurances refused to soak into Emma's heart. Maybe physically he was okay from his fall. But she wasn't okay. And neither was Cody. Not really. Not where it mattered. How could he be?

"It's my fault." All of it. No, most of it. There was a good bit that was still Max's fault.

But the fall was her fault.

She gripped the fence rail with both hands, aware of possibly gaining a splinter but unable to care. "I'm the one who had the bright idea to make the teens fall off chairs." Stupid, stupid, stupid. Exercises like that at church youth camps were one thing—but among a group of potentially reforming delinquents? What had she been thinking?

"It's not your fault." Max leaned in and parroted back everything she needed to hear, everything she would tell someone else if the roles were reversed, but she knew better. Deep down, she knew better. She should have seen this coming.

"We saw the way those guys acted on the blind-fold course." She spun around, not realizing he'd edged as close as he had. The stars provided a canopy of light across the darkness above his head, enveloping them in the still quiet that could only come from a ranch after hours. The kind of quiet she wanted to embrace and tuck into her soul and keep once she was back in the hectic bustle of Dallas.

Assuming she and Cody ever made it back in one piece.

"We had no idea they'd team up against him like that and let him fall." Max's brow tightened, probably remembering the same thing she had. After making sure Tonya was safely on the ground, Emma had run to Cody, only to find Max had beaten her there. He'd single-handedly shoved the teens back, helped Cody catch the breath that had been knocked out of him, and doled out punishment to the boys at fault.

While Emma stood back. Helpless.

Guilty.

Her stomach roiled. "I don't know why I'm here."

"You're here because you're needed." Max's answer came swiftly, as if he'd kept it ready for just such a declaration. "You can't control everything, Emma."

No kidding.

She rubbed her eyes with the palms of her hands. "Tonya's pregnant."

"Pregnant." He said the word as if it tasted bad, as if he wished he could spit it back out. She knew the feeling; she'd felt the same the first time she stared at two pink lines crawling up a tiny display window. He let out a huff of surprise. "Never thought I'd wish for an eating disorder instead."

"She confided in me after I caught her." Emma hitched herself up on the fence, tired of standing and carrying her own weight. She perched on the top rail, now face-to-face with Max. "I found the test in the bathroom."

Surprise flickered. "She didn't even try to hide it?"

"I think she knew it was a matter of time at that point." She'd held Tonya's braids back as the girl dry heaved in the bathroom later that evening after the trust exercises and promised her they'd figure it out. She was in for a long road.

Max sighed as if releasing the burdens of the entire world. "I'll have to call her parents in the morning. She can't stay here in that condition."

"I figured." She hated to let Tonya go, but this required a different level of care than Camp Hope could handle. Tonya needed counseling and support and a health plan. "I'm going to keep in touch with her."

"Of course." Max nodded as if he'd never expected less.

"Why do you believe in me so much?" The words left her lips in a whisper, and she half hoped he didn't hear.

He took her hand from the fence railing and

brought it to his lips for a quick kiss. "Because I know your heart."

She pulled her hand free. "No, you don't." If he did, if he really knew what lay beneath the surface, he'd run. Just like she'd run thirteen years ago. He'd hold against her everything she deserved for him to, and it would hurt. Worse maybe than it did a decade prior.

She wasn't strong enough to make it through that kind of pain a second time.

"Just because we haven't kept in contact over the years doesn't mean you've changed so much I don't know you." He tucked her hand between both of his, craning his head up slightly to speak into her eyes. "I've seen your heart for the girls. I've seen your heart for Cody. I've seen your heart for his freedom." His voice caught, and he looked away before taking her gaze hostage once again. "It's beautiful. You're making a difference."

"Some difference." She couldn't pull her hand away if she tried, but she didn't really want to. After her emotionally draining day, the human contact warmed a piece of her she wasn't sure she should thaw. "I didn't even realize Tonya was pregnant. It's so obvious now...."

"Hindsight is always clearer. You were great with her, and she trusted you. She showed us that over and over." Max rubbed his thumb across her knuckles. "You didn't have to confront her about the test. She came to you. That's huge."

True. And the trust exercise *was* a large part of what had prompted the confession. Maybe she hadn't completely lost her skill, but what did that say about Cody? Was it really that different just because she was his mom? Max had gotten through to him in ways she couldn't, and he was Cody's father.

But he didn't know.

Her chest tightened. Maybe that was the difference. If she confessed before the graduation, she could literally mess up Cody's entire progress. Before, it'd just been a fear and a gut instinct prompting her toward that decision. But now, it seemed more like proof. The odds were already stacked so high against Cody, and the fact that the kids were continually picking on him as the runt of the litter didn't help at all. It only urged him to prove himself harder and faster—with more rule breaking and chest thumping.

She really missed the days of superhero sheets and cracker crumbs and stepping on building blocks. They were alone, but they had each other, and life was so much easier. Back when only Emma knew what they were missing, and she could make it up to Cody in the form of ice cream cones and tent sleepovers.

Now she had nothing. Nothing to offer but a court ordered camp and a desperate arsenal of prayers.

Would it be enough?

"I want to start over." Max's confession blasted

like a shotgun in the silence of the star-studded night. "I want another chance."

She stared at him, mouth slightly open, all too aware of the responding pound of her heart.

Then before she could decide what to say, he broke the silence for her.

His mouth against hers was familiar in a bitter-sweet way, but the gentleness in his fingers threading through her hair was brand-new. So was the caution he exhibited as he kissed her, carefully, as though she was a treasure that might break. Gone was the selfishness from the touch she remembered years before. And in its place lingered something she wanted to hold on to forever.

She kissed him back with more than a decade's worth of longing, then turned away, her lips trailing across the stubble along his jaw. He let out a ragged breath in her ear, his hands gripping her waist firmly even as he pushed away, putting distance between them while keeping her balanced on the fence.

"I know you have your own life in Dallas." Max rested his forehead on hers, snuck another kiss, then backed away completely as if realizing he just couldn't get that close.

Own life. Dallas. Yes.

The fog cleared, and snatches of life—real life— pressed back to the surface. But she didn't want real life. She wanted to stay in this pocket of still-ness, where teen pregnancies and teen rebellion and life-altering secrets didn't exist. Where there was only the twinkle of the stars and the love in a certain cowboy's eyes and the whisper that life—her life—could still be different. Could be restored.

"But maybe…" His voice trailed, and he tucked a wisp of hair behind her ear. His touch burned a trail along her cheek and she shivered. "Maybe."

Maybe. So much potential in that word. So much hope. When was the last time she'd hoped? She wanted to hope. Wanted to feel again. To believe. To trust. Was it possible?

"Maybe." She breathed out the word, and the smile that started at the corners of his mouth let her know it hit its target. *Maybe* would have to be enough for now.

Maybe would hold back real life a little while longer.

She felt the exact same in his arms. Maybe better. Max couldn't believe he stood near a fence on his own property, hosting a ministry near to his heart and holding the hand of the one woman who'd branded him years ago as her own. He finally felt whole.

He squeezed Emma's hand, debating kissing her again but afraid he wouldn't want to stop. He took in her flushed cheeks and heavy-lidded eyes, and his breath caught. No, he definitely wouldn't want to stop. Some things never changed, but keeping any developing relationship under God's direction this time would be one thing they'd for sure do differently.

Better to get back to conversation. And maybe movement.

"Let's walk. Check on the horses." He extended his arm and Emma hopped down from the fence, linking her arm through his as they plodded through the shadows toward the barn.

"Caley said she enjoyed meeting you." He watched Emma's face carefully for her reaction, knowing how guarded she'd been around the firefighter earlier that morning. "The girls seemed to take to her. She said she'll be back."

She nodded, eyes cast on the ground as she dodged a hole. "Good. I think her talking to them about their careers is a great idea."

He did, too—though Tonya's immediate future was definitely altered at the moment. The reminder sobered Max's spirits. Still, the girl had clearly made her choices before she came to Camp Hope. It wasn't their fault, but they could still at least propel her on to the right course from here on out.

Which brought up another question.

"Why did Tonya's pregnancy hit you so hard?" He opened the door to the barn, and the automatic lights lit the sharp corners of the darkness.

"What do you mean?" A wall went up; he could see it climbing as tangibly as construction workers laid brick.

Oops. "Nothing. You just seemed to take it almost personally. I didn't want you thinking that was your fault, too."

Remington popped his head over the stall door, and Emma reached in and rubbed his mane. "It's a long story."

"I have all night." He crossed his arms and grinned, but the effect was wasted. Emma had officially launched into her own world, and she didn't seem to be issuing any invitations to join her. "You don't have to bear the burdens of the world, you know."

That got her attention. Her eyes narrowed, and the warmth between them began to cool. "You don't know a thing about my burdens."

"Whoa." He held up both hands in defense, causing Remington to toss his head and duck back into his stall. "I'm trying to help here."

"I know you are. But Cody is…impossible. He's not who he used to be." Emma turned to face him, tears glistening. "Not everything is an easy fix, you know. Not Tonya. Not Cody. And not—" She stopped herself, and he'd have given his back forty acres to know what she'd been about to say.

He tried a different approach. "I never said it was easy. Cody is just tired of being treated like a textbook. He wants a mom, not a counselor."

Her eyes widened as if she'd been struck, and his heart shifted toward his boots. He'd said too much—crossed a camper confidentiality line, and at probably the worst possible time.

He tried to backtrack. "Emma, I'm on your side." He reached out to touch her, but she didn't soften. If anything, she grew stonier. This was not what he'd intended to do. "I just meant it's not all your responsibility."

"So whose is it?" Her eyes flashed. "Who *is* responsible for wayward kids? Whose fault is it?"

"Fault?" They'd gotten way off topic, but clearly this was something Emma had been keeping just below the surface. As much as he'd wanted to know what was going on in her head, he wasn't sure he could handle this much roller coaster. Not tonight, with the weight of the day still pressing in. He struggled to take a breath against the heaviness suddenly covering the barn. "Why does it have to be anyone's fault? Stuff happens. Kids are influenced or hurt and no one can necessarily prevent—"

"But some can. Some can be prevented. And in those cases, there *is* someone to blame."

She believed a lie, and it was killing her. His heart softened at her burden. "You're not to blame, Emma. There's no way."

Her lips pressed together but didn't contain the words that exploded forth like a shot from his favorite rifle. "You're right. I'm not." The tears spilled over, leaving makeup speckled trails down her cheeks. "You are."

Chapter Seventeen

She'd said it. There was no turning back now.

But that didn't stop her from hightailing it out of the barn.

Emma picked up her pace, the ground rising to trip her, but she kept going, stumbling in the darkness toward the light shining in the main house's front window. Her outburst raced through her head almost as fast as her legs churned the ground, and she mentally railed on herself. How could she have said that? Thirteen years of keeping a secret, down the drain. She never should have told her mom. That unplugged the dam, and now she was about to pay for over a decade of silence.

Max didn't let escape come easily.

He caught up in a few quick strides and grabbed her arm. She pulled him along, knowing he was too stubborn to let go, yet too much of a gentleman to force her to stop. "Emma, wait. What do you mean?"

He had to know by now, typo or not. Did he really *not* get it? The possibility that he didn't brought hope, but it was tainted with instant disappointment. She either had to lie to his face, or confess. Neither option felt right.

She stopped just inside the front door, and Max finally released her as if realizing she had nowhere else to go.

And she didn't. Her past had finally caught up to her, right there in a dimly lit living room on a ranch in the middle of Broken Bend, Louisiana. A ranch for troubled teens. *Their* troubled teen.

"I know you're angry. But I don't really get why." Max stepped back to give her room—or maybe give himself room—and tossed his cowboy hat on the table by the door. His rumpled hair just made him all the more endearing, and the memory of their kiss seared her lips. What had she been thinking, saying "maybe" like that? As if they actually had a chance? As if this bomb of a truth she was about to detonate wouldn't change anything? Change everything?

Out. Of. Her. Mind.

"Talk to me, Emma." His tone pitched at the end, revealing his desperation, and it almost broke the shield around her heart. He cared—really cared.

But not for long.

"Why are you mad? Was it the kiss?" He was starting to look angry now, too, probably because she couldn't make herself speak. Her mind wouldn't shut up, but her lips refused to open and say what she'd buried for so long. "I'm sorry if I rushed you. If it was too—"

"That's not it." There, finally, her voice. She held up her hand, wanting to touch him but knowing it'd just be pouring fuel on the fire she was about to light. "The kiss was…well. It was." Wonderful. Perfect. Everything she'd missed since their last one years ago. But the desire seeped and soaked underneath layers of bitterness she thought she'd rid herself of, yet apparently, had only been hiding.

"What's my fault?" He stabbed his fingers through his hair, drawing the rumples even higher. "I don't get it, Emma. I was trying to reassure you that Cody's choices aren't your fault, and you spin it around on me? You know I've done nothing but try to help him this entire time. And he's making progress. I don't understand why you're so—"

"You're right. You don't understand." Her stomach cramped. "There's something you don't know." She wanted to pray, wanted to beg God to take this situation away, just make it disappear—but there was no way. This was her choice. Her sin. Her consequences.

Coming full circle.

Hadn't she paid enough?

"If there's a missing puzzle piece here, then please, by all means fill me in." He spread his arms to the side, his expression as haphazard as his hair.

Guilt shook her insides. She'd pushed him to his

own limit, what with their exhausting day, their kiss and half-spoken declarations, and now her random—in his eyes, at least—freak-out.

He stilled and lowered his voice. "I told you from the beginning the more I know about these campers and their home lives and their backgrounds, the better equipped I am to make a difference."

"You made a difference all right." Ah. *There* was her alternating archenemy and best friend, Resentment, bubbling to the surface. She could psychoanalyze herself down to her own core, but somehow, she felt helpless to put into practice the advice she'd give her clients. This was too deep.

His eyes narrowed. "Quit with the riddles, Emma. Shoot straight."

Straight? Fine. Right to his heart. "You're Cody's dad."

Max had never told anyone this before, not even Brady, but he'd always secretly enjoyed the story of *Alice in Wonderland*. He'd discovered it in school, when a librarian read it to his class over a series of afternoons, and he'd carried those images with him for life. There was something appealing about it—though at the time, he'd not been masculine enough to admit it—about falling into an alternate reality, where cats grinned, and rabbits carried watches, and flamingos served as croquet mallets. Where nothing was as it seemed. Where anything could be possible—like finding a father who actually cared.

He never thought about how Alice must have felt tumbling down the hole to get there.

He knew now.

"Cody's dad." The words stuck on his tongue like they belonged to someone else. And maybe they did. How was this even possible? His mind raced with a reasonable argument, but all he could sputter was time. "Thirteen years. Thirteen years ago?"

"Right. Do the math."

He *had*.

And it hadn't added up. After he'd counted, all he'd focused on was Cody's explanation. *My dad was a jerk who left my mom when she was pregnant.*

How could—

Him? He was the jerk?

Heat spread across his cheeks and jaw and into his ears. "The birthday in his file doesn't—"

She swallowed, looked away. "It's a typo."

A typo. Everything, his entire life, and future, and past, boiled down to a typo.

What if she'd never admitted it? He'd have never known.

Because of a typo.

But black ink on paper or not, the truth remained. She'd lied. To both of them.

An ache started deep within as the realization of all he'd missed paraded before his eyes. He never got to feel his son kick. Never got to hold Emma's hand in the delivery room, never got to pose for a picture beside his newborn. Never got to help him potty train or take him to the doctor for checkups. Never got to watch Saturday cartoons or ride a bike.

Nothing.

Because of her.

"How could you?" He didn't recognize his own voice. Couldn't control its timbre. Couldn't stop the boiling rush of emotion rising in his throat and taking over. He slammed his fist against the door frame, and the wood cracked. "How could you!"

She didn't flinch. Didn't shake. Didn't even blink. Just stood there and took it—as if she knew she deserved it. Well, good. She did. How dare she stand there and tell him Cody's behavior was his fault when he hadn't even been there? Hadn't ever been given a choice?

His hand hurt.

Not as much as his heart.

The room felt as though it was caving in. Walls coming closer. He closed his eyes and shoved his fingers through his hair, his chest burning with unnamed feelings and regrets. And yet, underneath all of that…one question remained. "Why?"

If anything, her grip around herself tightened. "I did what I had to do."

"Oh, right. You *had* to run away and keep a secret." He laughed, a harsh sound void of amusement, one that rippled up from his churning stomach. "That makes perfect sense."

"Max, it's not like that." She reached out, but

he jerked away as if her touch would poison him. Maybe it already had. Maybe that was the source of his ache the past decade-plus—the effect of Emma and her secrets. Her selfishness. "You don't understand."

"You're right. I don't." He grabbed his hat and shoved it back on his head. "I'll never understand how you could keep a secret like that. How you could bring your son—*our* son—to my camp and still not tell me the truth." His voice rose with every new word. "How you could stand there and blame me for his choices, how you could kiss—" His breath caught and he hardened his heart. No. No tears. She certainly hadn't spent the past decade crying over him.

He wouldn't waste another solitary one on her. "Forget it." He wrenched open the door.

Her fingers brushed his sleeve. "Max, wait."

The door shook the frame as it slammed behind him, drowning out her protests.

Drowning out his own.

Emma curled up on her bed, trying to silence her sobs so as not to wake Tonya, Katie and Stacy. Her cell phone glowed on her nightstand, revealing that only seven minutes had passed since she'd last checked. Since time had decided to all but stand still. Since sleep continued to elude her.

Though that could be a blessing, since her dreams wouldn't be much better than reality.

She twisted on her back, scrunching her pillow under her head and brushing at the wet spot left from tears. It wasn't the first time she'd cried herself to sleep—or tried to—over Max Ringgold. But these tears stemmed from somewhere previously untapped.

And were oddly mixed with a small, yet very tangible, sense of relief.

It was done. Her all-too-familiar burden had been lifted, though a new one had immediately settled in its place. The secret was out. It was over. She could take a breath, a full breath, for the first time in too many years to count.

But they still had to tell Cody.

The relief vanished, and fresh tears soaked onto the neckline of her sleep shirt. And she thought telling Max had been hard? What was she thinking? She wasn't. Hadn't. But no, her plan used to make sense, back when it was just her and Cody, when she knew that there was zero chance of running into Max, zero chance for anything to change.

Yet everything *had* changed, and no one told her. *Because you never gave anyone a chance to.*

Her conscience reared, sharp and ugly and all too honest. She flopped on her side, the wet pillowcase sticking to her cheek. All these years, she'd convinced herself Cody's problems were Max's fault. If Max hadn't passed on those genes, if Max hadn't lived the way he'd lived, if Max hadn't done drugs, Cody would be different. If Max, if Max, if Max.

If Emma.

Now her conscience sounded a whole lot more like the Lord, another voice she'd squelched over the years of doing everything for herself. She'd been running from more than Max and her past. She'd been running from herself.

And her faith.

"I'm tired of running," she muttered into her pillow, and across the dorm, one of the girls shifted in her bed, sheets rustling. She stilled, trying to calm her pounding heartbeat, and uttered the words she should have spoken to God years ago. "I'm done running."

A slight pocket of peace began to envelop her, and she nestled into it like a downy quilt. Cody's problems weren't Max's fault. And they weren't hers. They were probably a little bit of both—but they were mostly Cody's. Maybe he'd been reacting in a way that connected to Emma's bad choices, but he was still ultimately responsible for himself. Just as she was. Just as Max was.

Of the three of them, Emma's choices might just be the worst. Hers didn't involve drugs and gangs. But she'd kept her choices and sins a secret. Max had always lived out loud, had never hidden who he claimed to be. He'd definitely made wrong decisions, but hadn't she? At least Max hadn't pretended to be something he wasn't.

She'd been pretending for thirteen years.

Another weight lifted, and her body relaxed even

as her heart sought to rid itself of her years of guilt and regret. She prayed honestly for the first time in too long, turning Cody over to the Lord and embracing the fact that for once, not having control over a situation might just be a good thing. The best thing.

For all of them.

Chapter Eighteen

Max managed to avoid Emma most of the following day, making an extra effort to keep the boys' and girls' schedules separate. He could go about Monday business as usual, as long as he didn't have to look at her. Luke had come in for the afternoon, since Nicole was resting and stable, and offered to take over with the campers while Max arranged for Tonya's parents to pick her up. He still couldn't believe he had a pregnant teen, a lying ex-girlfriend and a secret son on the premises.

His beloved camp had morphed into a low-budget soap opera.

He hung up the phone with Tonya's parents and ran his hand down his jaw. He felt old. Tired. And borderline useless. Not exactly the way he should be feeling as the end of the camp approached. He'd been so sure this would be the best session ever, yet it was shaping up to be an utter failure.

Did God want him to even do this ministry anymore?

He picked up his Bible, tried to quiet the rustlings in his heart, but he couldn't hear past the layer of anger. It was too raw, too fresh. He just hurt on too many levels—it was as though Emma betrayed him all over again. He'd dealt with the pain of losing her so suddenly, her rash change of mind that now, looking back, made sense. She hadn't wanted to have a child with him, so she'd bailed. Never looked back.

Until she'd been forced to.

Had the kiss they'd shared last night been real on her part, or more lies? He might never know—and it didn't really matter. It wasn't as if there could be a repeat with this huge barrier between them. No wonder she'd been so guarded in her time at the ranch. The fact that she'd even taken the job he offered was huge. Maybe she'd been seeking to make amends in her own way, knowing she owed him. But no, that wasn't Emma. Emma wasn't the type to strive to right wrongs.

That was more his style.

He tucked his Bible back into his desk drawer. No number of Psalms would stop the incessant roiling of his thoughts today. He'd read later when he could make sense of the words beyond his own heartbeat.

He was a dad. A *father*. He had a son.

It still didn't make sense, though the uncanny

connection he felt to Cody now rang clear. The similarities, the matching stubbornness. That deep desire to help him that went beyond what he'd ever felt toward a camper before.

His son.

How was he supposed to act around Cody? How could he look at the boy the same? Impossible. He couldn't—nor should he. But when would they tell him? Had Emma even considered the ramifications of *that?*

He almost wished she'd kept her secret a couple weeks longer.

Max groaned. He wasn't ready for this. He had no training of his own to be a dad, no example. Look what his own father had been and how Max had turned out. Maybe he'd made it eventually through the worst, but the earlier years…well, he still had a lot of making up to do. A lot to prove. To himself, and to God.

What if he messed up Cody even further?

Max shoved away from his desk, the chair squeaking against the floor, and moved to turn off his office light. He couldn't dwell on that right now, not when he'd have to see Cody soon and be forced to keep up Emma's charade a bit longer. He had to focus on business for the time being. People depended on him—like Tonya. Her parents would be there by the end of the day, so he needed to tell her to get her things ready.

He tucked the folded slip of paper recommending

professional counseling into his shirt pocket and made a mental note to hand it over to her family when they arrived. Hopefully she'd find the right path and stay on it. He could sort of commiserate now with Emma's misplaced guilt over the girl. Tonya had such potential—but she'd been keeping a secret, too. He couldn't help what he wasn't aware of.

Which begged the question—what else didn't he know about his campers?

It was enough to make a man paranoid.

He started for the kitchen to grab a bottle of water, then ducked back out at the sound of Mama Jeanie's singing. She always sang when she cooked, and he didn't want to listen to the hymns right now, nor did he want another lecture full of cryptic wisdom. Just couldn't stomach it today.

He turned up the stairs to his master bedroom, thinking to grab some water from the dorm fridge he kept by his bed instead, and paused at what sounded suspiciously like footsteps—on the second floor, where no campers were allowed. He frowned, quickening his step and pushing open the door to his room with authority.

No one was there.

Probably just the floorboards creaking. The house wasn't exactly new.

He grabbed a bottle of water from the fridge and twisted open the lid. He took a long sip, then replaced the cap as a sinking sensation spread through his gut. Something was different. He turned a slow circle in the center of the room, trying to place it. The rug on the wood floor by the dresser lay flat and straight. The dark green bedspread still hung crooked like he'd left it—as usual, since the only reason he made his bed in the first place was because he enforced that rule with the campers. The rustic clock of a cowboy knelt before a cross ticked a steady rhythm, the only sound breaking the quiet. He shrugged. All was right.

Except he hadn't left his top dresser drawer open an inch.

He tossed the bottle down and pulled the drawer open. Should be socks. Boxers. And…he fished underneath the rolls of wadded socks. It wasn't there.

Oh, no.

He slammed the drawer shut just as an angry voice sounded from behind.

Cody, red-faced and steely-eyed, stood framed in the doorway, holding the picture of Max and Emma. "You're a liar."

Emma woke with a remnant of the peace she'd found the night before but not all of it. She went through the motions of the day, trying to focus on the girls and their activities, realizing her remaining time with Tonya was short, but she couldn't shake the memory of Max's face when she'd confessed.

Finally, she couldn't take it any longer. She had

to see Max, had to know how he was processing this, or she'd explode with the what-ifs. She left the girls with Faith in the barn, saddling up for a trail ride under Luke's direction, and headed for the main house.

Mama Jeanie intercepted her outside the kitchen before the door even shut behind her. "Don't go upstairs." Her tone, always brisk and authoritative, seemed even firmer than usual.

Emma hesitated. "Where's Max?"

"Upstairs." Mama Jeanie shifted the mixing bowl she held in one hand to the other, pausing to swipe her free arm against her apron. "You're not going on the trail ride?" She gestured out the front window, where Luke, Faith and Tim were monitoring the teens as they buckled saddle girths.

"Maybe later. Right now I need to find Max." Not that it was any of Mama Jeanie's business. The woman had a kind heart, but Emma wasn't in the mood for instruction from someone who had no idea the level of chaos they were currently in. She headed for the stairs.

Mama Jeanie's voice neared panic. "I don't think right now is a good time."

Sudden yelling sounded from above, punctuated by a slamming door and thumping footsteps. Emma's heart raced as she stared with dread up the staircase. Had Max totally lost it? She looked back at Mama Jeanie, her former irritation long gone as she considered hiding behind the petite woman.

Max had never had a temper like that—in fact, that sounded more like how Cody used to—

Cody pounded down the stairs, almost flying past her, but she reached out with long-honed instincts and caught the sleeve of his sweatshirt. "Not so fast. Where are you going?"

He spun in a sudden half circle at her interception, and something small and square fluttered from his grip and landed at her feet.

Emma stared down at her own image, arms curled around Max's shoulder, a happy grin on her face as he pressed a kiss against her temple, and dread seeped through her chest. She released Cody's sleeve, staring in horror at the proof she couldn't deny. No. No. No. Why had Max kept that? So many years ago…the implications bubbled to the surface and layered her dread with regret. He'd waited for her.

She was going to be sick.

Max appeared on the bottom steps moments later, out of breath but not heaving nearly as hard as Cody. "Cody, wait." His "I'm in charge" voice did nothing to defuse the situation. "I know you're upset, but we've got to talk about this."

"Talk about what?" The teen bent and snatched the photo from the ground, waving it in their faces. *"Dad."*

Emma sucked in her breath, and Max's face drained of color. He hadn't told him. Cody had figured it out? How?

It was as if he read her mind.

"Yeah, I might get in trouble a lot, but I'm not stupid." He pointed at Max. "Everyone kept telling me how much you looked like me. How we talked the same. Same stupid cowlick." He slapped at his hair.

"Why were you in my room, Cody?" A slow flush of red filled Max's throat and jaw.

"Looking for cash." He stuck his chin out in contrived bravado, but the slight quiver gave away his emotion. "On a dare."

"From who?"

"What's it matter? I found this instead. I didn't steal." His eyes, glassy with unshed tears, narrowed at Max. "You lied to me. Made me think you were on my side. And, Mom…you…" His voice grew smaller and the betrayal in his eyes shattered Emma's heart. "You lied the most. The longest."

"We need to talk." Max held out his hand. "Give me the picture, Cody."

From the corner of her eye, she observed Mama Jeanie slipping quietly back into the kitchen, giving them space. She wished she could follow her. Emma knew what Max was doing, trying to defuse the situation by establishing control, by prompting Cody to respond to them in obedience in a small matter to build trust toward the bigger issue. Handing over the picture was the first step to them all calming down and restoring the proper order.

Not that it'd be that easy.

"Fine. You want it?" Cody picked up the photo, ripped it in half and tossed the pieces at them. "Take it. I don't want it. Don't want either of you."

The door slammed behind him, and something unleashed deep inside Emma, cracking open and revealing even more shattered pieces. Her son was done with her. Because of Max.

Her peace from the night before disappeared completely into a dark abyss of hopelessness. "This *is* your fault." She poked her finger hard against Max's chest. "You did this! You kept that picture. You passed down all of this anger and rebellion. It's you!"

"It takes two people to make a child, Emma." Max gripped her forearms and held her away from him. "You're the one that left, that never even gave me a chance to be involved!"

"How could I? I came back, Max. I came back!" She struggled in his grip, all logic and reasoning fleeing her senses as she surrendered herself to the pent-up emotion she'd restrained for far too long. "I saw you making that deal." The words hissed from her lips, words she'd been longing to fling at him for thirteen years.

"What deal?" Confusion and pain seeped from his expression, despite his voice rising even louder than hers. But instead of anger, it was laced with panic. "I don't know what you're talking about!"

"The drugs, Max. You said you would quit. That I was enough." Her voice shook with unshed sobs and she struggled to get the words out through the tears. "I saw you taking that deal. At the park. Near our spot."

Clarity bled through Max's eyes, and he released Emma's arms abruptly. "I flushed those."

She staggered backward. "What?"

He stabbed his fingers through his hair. "I flushed them. I did the deal, yeah. I was weak. I missed you and wanted a distraction. But the second he left, I remembered my promise to you and that meant more to me than a temporary fix. I never did a hit after the last one you knew about, Emma. I flushed them."

He'd flushed them.

And he'd changed.

Yet she'd ran.

Despair began a slow assault, pummeling her heart. She reached toward Max, but it was like stretching toward the past—impossible to grasp.

"I didn't know." The words sounded impossibly weak, and the biggest understatement anyone had ever spoken.

The grief in his eyes would linger in her memory for the rest of her days. "You didn't let me tell you."

The back door burst open, and Luke ran in, hair mussed and jacket flapping open. "Cody and Jarvis are gone."

"Gone? What do you mean?" Max strode past Luke to the porch, scanning both directions. "He was just here."

"There was a mix up. We split up the group for the trail ride, and Tim and I both thought Cody was with the other group. We didn't get far before realizing we didn't have Cody or Jarvis with us. They're not in the dorms, either, or the rec room." Luke's eyes filled with worry. "I think they ran away."

Chapter Nineteen

Not even twenty-four hours into fatherhood, and Max had lost his son.

He paced in front of the barn, wishing there was something else he could do besides walk and watch his breath puff as the afternoon waned colder. Tim and Faith had gone back out to finish the trail ride with the rest of the campers, in an effort to keep them in the dark about what was going on a little while longer. Luke called in backup from the church for a search party, while Tonya's parents picked her up not a minute too soon. Emma had hugged the girl goodbye on the porch, then disappeared inside the dormitory. He didn't know what she was doing. Packing? Pacing? Praying?

Would she leave?

Did he want her to?

Thankfully Brady, Caley and Ava had come over right away. After quick hugs, the girls went to the kitchen to help Mama Jeanie make some refreshments for the search crew while Brady followed his pace.

"It's going to be okay, man. We'll find them." Brady rubbed his hands together before pulling his gloves from his jacket pocket.

"He's my son."

Brady stopped midstep, one glove dangling from his fingers. "Say what?"

"Cody's my kid. Emma told me last night." He shoved his hands in his pockets, not having any gloves to wear and grateful for the cold ache in his fingers that reminded him he wasn't totally numb after all. Yet.

Brady's hand clamped his shoulder. "We'll figure this out. Nothing's too big for the Lord." He offered a wry grin. "Not even this kind of a secret."

Max snorted. "Guess we'll see." If they found them, that is. Jarvis and Cody together were an unlikely pair, and Max couldn't figure out what they were up to. Why would the two kids who hated each other the most run off together? To create trouble? To fight it out alone? That didn't seem like Cody's style, though the anger that had radiated off him when he left the house earlier hadn't, either. The kid's—his *son's*—wounds ran deep.

Mostly because of him and Emma and their mistakes.

"Search party's ready. We're going to split up and spread out." Luke strode to Max's side and gestured to the group of men behind him, wearing jackets and ball caps, some with walkie-talkies clipped to their belts. Max recognized most of them from the church, though there were new faces, as well. Ten men in all.

"Thanks for coming." They made a quick plan to determine groups and who would search where. Most would go on foot, while one set took the remaining horses from the barn, and another took his and Brady's four-wheelers. Some would take the road, though that was the least likely way the boys would have traveled.

Luke stepped closer to Max and lowered his voice. "Have you called the police?"

"Not yet." Max rubbed his jaw. "Trying to avoid that if possible. But if they get too far…" His property spread a good ways, but the worst part was, it joined with Brady's. It wouldn't take the boys any effort to shimmy under the fence and then have free rein for miles on the Double C—including bulls and wild animals. "Let's see what we find first." Just couldn't wait too long, because once it got dark, the boys were in for a rough night. In some ways it'd teach them a valuable lesson, but Max hoped to avoid lessons involving coyotes—or worse. Besides, his campers' parents trusted him to keep them safe.

The sight of Brady's pistol tucked into the back of his jeans as he hurried off only made the reality of their situation more grim.

The men left, agreeing Max would stay at Camp Hope to be there for the campers when the trail ride ended. He had to keep things running, whether he felt like it or not. Suddenly alone, he stared down at the path he'd created in the dirt while pacing and slowly began to rub the evidence away with his boot. Too bad he couldn't erase the past twenty-four hours as easily.

But what would he change? He couldn't go back to pretending he didn't have a kid. The thought now brought a hollow ache to his gut. There were some things the heart couldn't un-know. He would be there for Cody from here on out, no matter what. But what would that look like? They lived in different worlds. His work was at Camp Hope, in the nowhere town of Broken Bend, Louisiana, while Emma and Cody had their own life in a big thriving Texas city.

So many questions. So few answers.

And none of them would matter if Cody didn't make it back in one piece.

Panic, the kind Max realized only a father could feel, seized his heart. He began to pray. *God, I can't fix this. I don't know where my son is, but You do. Could You show us, please?* He began to pace again, this time praying with every footstep. There was nothing he could do about the past—he couldn't get back the time he'd lost, the time Emma had robbed him of. But he could pray for the future.

And despite his lingering anger and betrayal over Emma's choices, he wanted a future with them. As a family.

It seemed too impossible to even pray for.

Was that what a father's love did? Sought the impossible? Hoped when there was little or no proof to do so?

His father hadn't shown him that kind of love.

But his Heavenly Father had.

And he'd ignored it. Shoved it away. Sought to prove himself against the grace freely offered to him.

He stopped pacing. Just like he loved Cody regardless of this bad choice he'd made, regardless of Cody's sin and rebellion, God loved *him* the same way, plus some. He didn't have to strive to make up for the past, to make up for his own years of rebellion and sin—he'd already been forgiven. Just like he'd already forgiven Cody for running away.

And just like he needed to forgive Emma.

Her feeble protests racked his brain. *I did what I had to do.* She really did. He tried to put himself in her shoes. Pregnant, scared, uncertain. Coming back to Broken Bend to announce the biggest news of her life, when her parents didn't even know they'd been *dating,* and discovering her baby's father buying drugs.

Wouldn't he have been tempted to run, too?

Empathy began to replace the judgment he'd

been holding, and it bled through his heart. They'd all made bad choices.

But that didn't mean there wasn't room for a second chance.

There were some regrets even raw cookie dough couldn't touch.

From her spot on the bar stool in the kitchen, Emma breathed in the aroma of chocolate chip cookies wafting from Mama Jeanie's oven, yet the smell just made her sick. Her son was out there, somewhere, with another teen who was nothing but trouble, and all she knew for sure was that Cody hated her. She buried her face in her hands. She'd tried to join the search party, but Max interfered, stating Cody would be more likely to hide if he saw her coming. True—painfully true.

"Don't worry. They're going to find them." Caley wrapped her arm around Emma's shoulders and rubbed. "They're good men. Some are volunteer firemen—they know what they're doing."

Emma nodded, refusing to lift her head, afraid to look at anyone for fear of breaking down and never stopping. A drawer opened and shut, and Mama Jeanie mumbled to Caley about taking Ava to help set out the cups for the cider she'd made.

The door shut behind them, and Emma finally dared to look up at Caley. "I'm an idiot." The whole story poured from her lips, and Caley didn't move or interrupt except to don an oven mitt and remove the cookies.

"Sounds to me like you're getting smarter." She turned off the oven and grinned. "Seriously, don't be so hard on yourself. You're aware of what went wrong, and you want to fix it. That's a lot farther than some people ever get." She took the bar stool beside Emma and tossed the mitt on the counter. "Trust me. You guys are going to be fine. When Brady and I were getting together—man, it was rough. I didn't think we'd ever find a way around our differences."

Emma shoved away from the counter, holding up both hands in defense. "No, no, no. This is different. I'm not getting back with Max."

Caley winked. "Yet."

"How can you be so sure?" Her heart began to pound again, and this time it had nothing to do with the fact that her son was missing or she'd just ruined a good man's life with her selfishness. "He'll never forgive me. And he shouldn't."

"Yes, he should. And he will. I know Max." Caley hopped up and began scooping cookies from the sheet onto a plate. "He might nurse this wound a little while, but he'll do the right thing."

The right thing. As in, obligation? No thanks. She'd run from that once already, which was why she didn't tell her parents about her and Max in the first place. No shotgun weddings in her past—or her future—even if Max held the proverbial gun this time. She didn't want obligation. She wanted love.

But she'd ruined it.

Like she'd ruined Cody.

"They found them!" Ava's excited teenaged voice shot through the silence of the kitchen, and Caley dropped the spatula on the stove. Emma shot off her stool, hope breaking through the depression and taking over like a beacon in the night. She raced onto the porch in time to see Brady leading Cody toward Max, who eagerly ran to meet them across the yard. Joy burst free deep in her chest. She took three steps off the porch, then hesitated at the anger in Cody's expression as he shoved Max's arm away.

This wasn't the prodigal son returning.

Luke began dispatching into the walkie-talkies to end the search, then stopped, his finger still on the button as static burst from the contraption. "Wait. Hold that thought. Where's Jarvis?"

All eyes landed on Cody, who stared stubbornly at the ground and shrugged.

Max shut the door of his office and perched on the side of his desk as Cody slumped into a chair. "So what's my punishment?" He scowled.

He was in no way equipped for this. Any other camper, yes. But his own son? Not even close. Max briefly closed his eyes, wishing there were a handbook, a class, a conference he could have attended to know what to do in this case.

But it was just him and Cody.

And the Lord.

He breathed a prayer for guidance and clasped his hands in front of him. "There's still a bigger issue at hand than punishment right now, Cody. That's going to have to wait."

"Great." Cody shifted away from Max, his body language loud and clear.

Max took the seat beside him, wanting to appear less imposing, and cleared his throat. "We need to know where Jarvis is."

"How should I know?" He stared at the bookcase lining the wall beside him, eyes flickering between the titles.

Max took a deep breath and let it out slowly. He couldn't afford to show anger. He at least knew enough to realize that wouldn't help. Cody was hurting, and he was lashing out because he didn't think he had any other options.

"You both disappeared at the same time. Are you telling me you weren't together?" He stared at Cody, wishing he could break the barrier between them with something tangible. No wonder Emma felt so frustrated for so long. She was a professional, and she couldn't reach her own son. Rather, she was stuck watching him spiral downward in a cycle she was helpless to stop.

It hurt like nothing else did.

Cody met his eyes, and something shifted slightly. He didn't want to lie to his face, and that spoke more of the good in the boy's heart than anything else since his arrival at camp. They'd connected before, and Cody was remembering. He could see it in his gaze. If only he'd remember Max wasn't the bad guy....

"We left together." Cody grudgingly admitted the truth. "But that's all I know."

"I don't think it is."

Cody snorted. "You're calling *me* a liar? Sort of ironic."

He'd have a point, though Cody didn't know Max hadn't known about their relationship until hours before he'd discovered it, too. But how could Max tell him that now without throwing Emma under the bus? Oh, it was tempting. He wanted that bond with Cody, wanted to see forgiveness in his eyes more than he'd ever wanted anything else. Wanted to take that first step toward a real relationship of trust.

But he wouldn't sacrifice Emma to do so.

A knock sounded on his shut office door, and then it swung open before he could respond. Emma stepped inside, her face a fixed mask of determination. "It's not Max's fault. And yes, I was listening at the door."

His mouth opened a little. Gone was the meek, unsure Emma he'd seen around Cody in the past. In its place stood mama-bear Emma, whose claws were out and teeth were sharp—ready to do what was necessary regardless of the cost. "Your dad isn't the liar, Cody. I am."

His admiration for Emma grew ten leaps. She was finally stepping up.

"Yeah, right. How can I believe that you're even telling the truth now?" Cody stood up, his voice rising, but Max gently sat him back down with a firm hand on his shoulder.

"I think you should listen to your mom." His tone left little room for argument, and even Cody knew it.

He slumped and crossed his arms, redirecting his gaze to the floor. "Whatever."

Emma came around and stood directly in front of him. "I kept the secret, Cody. It was my fault, not your father's."

Cody's lips rolled in at the word *father,* and Max felt his own insides tremble a little.

"We were a couple, a long time ago, when I was leaving for college. I found out then I was expecting you." Emma took a deep breath. "Your dad didn't know until last night."

Cody's eyes darted to meet hers, surprise replacing the previous sullen stare. "Are you serious? You didn't even tell *him?*" Judgment sprang forth, the same judgment Max had felt hours before.

Now it was his turn to do the right thing.

"Your mom did what she thought she had to do. It's a long story, and it's complicated and between us adults." Max leaned forward, bracing his elbows on his knees. "But bottom line—she made her choice because she loved you and wanted what was best for you." He hesitated. "Once upon a time, Cody, I was definitely not what was best for you. Or your mom."

He'd finally admitted that out loud, and the truth brought his own measure of much-needed freedom—and possibilities. Could it be possible that God's timing really was perfect? That if somehow Emma had pushed past her own instincts and morals, and made a life with him right away when she'd come home, that he wouldn't have made it where he was now? Maybe if he'd had Emma and everything he'd wanted right away, he wouldn't have grown closer to the Lord as he had in those tumultuous years. Wouldn't have started Camp Hope. Wouldn't have the message and testimony that had changed so many lives.

He didn't know for sure, and never would. But he believed that God hadn't left them—any of them—in the meantime. And that good was being worked regardless.

Cody's gaze bounced back and forth between them, as if feeling out their sincerity. Then the hardness cracked, and he licked his lips, a hitch in his voice. "I didn't mean that, Mom. About, you know…not wanting you."

She quickly closed her eyes as a tear slipped down her cheek. "I know."

Max wished he could hug her, or better yet,

somehow prompt Cody to, but that would come. This elephant was going to take a bite at a time. At least Cody seemed off the ledge now, and maybe he'd finally find some healing and move forward.

With both of them.

"I don't know why I'm the way I am." Cody's voice, so timid now, was nearly lost in the hum of the heater. "I just don't want to do this anymore."

Emma stiffened. "Do what?"

"You know…the bad stuff. Getting in trouble. It started out just trying to make friends. Be accepted." He sniffed, his jaw set. "It got out of control. And I couldn't stop. I had to keep up."

"You don't have to keep up anymore, Cody." Max shifted forward, heart full. "You can start making better choices today. You don't have to go home the same." He hesitated. "It just takes work, son. Are you ready to do the work now?"

Suddenly, Cody sprang to his feet, but not with the eagerness Max had hoped he'd show. No, this expression was nothing if not sheer panic. "Wait. You've got to find Jarvis!"

"That's what we've been trying to tell you." Max stood as well, trying to switch gears as abruptly as Cody had. "Do you know where he is?"

"No. We split up once we cleared the property line. But you've got to find him!" Cody pointed outside with fear in his eyes. "He's going to start a fire."

Chapter Twenty

Emma didn't even have time to bask in the longed-for moment of Cody's breakthrough. She followed Max and Cody outside as Max rushed to use a walkie-talkie to alert Luke to Jarvis's plan. Her son felt so good tucked under her arm—it seemed as though she hadn't been able to touch him in months, despite their goodbye hug the first day of camp. She squeezed him a little tighter on instinct, and he leaned slightly into her embrace before regaining his usual stance.

She'd take what she could get, and she'd love every second of it.

There were still too many pressing questions hounding her mind. What now? What next? But she refused to answer any of them, determined to be content to just stand beside her son and watch the chaos unfold before her as news spread about Jarvis's plans.

Max jogged back toward them. "Cody, do you

know where he was going to start the fire?" His eyes were wide with concern, yet his stature confident as Brady and the lingering men filed in behind him. A rush of emotion spread through Emma's stomach. She would have never dreamed that Max—*her* Max—would one day exhibit such desirable traits, would one day be in charge and leading a worthwhile group rather than following the lead of others with ill intent.

But he wasn't hers anymore.

The emotion morphed to pain. Maybe there was something to be said for God's timing, but it was too late for her and Max. She needed to put any hope of such craziness out of her mind immediately, or she might never recover. She still had to focus on her and Cody, and doing what was best for her son.

Even if that meant leaving Broken Bend for the second time.

Max spoke in a clipped tone into Luke's walkie-talkie, then handed it back. "We're going to have to spread out again. He could be planning to hit the dorms, or anywhere in the forest, or—"

A sudden orange glow filled the window of the stables, and Emma's heart jump-started. "Or the barn."

Max jerked his head toward the stables, and his confident demeanor vanished. "Fire!"

Immediately, the men on the property sprang into action. Brady called 9-1-1 while Max and the others ran toward the barn and began hauling hay, buckets and other miscellaneous objects away from the perimeter. Thankfully the barn was empty of animals since all of the horses were on the trail ride or on the search party.

Tires squealed, and Emma looked in time to see Caley peeling out of the driveway in Brady's truck, gassing it toward the road.

"Where's she going?" Cody craned his head, but the only thing that remained was the dust stirred from the sudden departure.

"She's a volunteer firefighter. I bet she's going to get her gear." She held Cody close, and this time, he didn't pull away as more flames began to lick the sides of the barn, threatening to devour the structure in a mass of gold, tangerine and crimson light.

"I didn't mean for this to happen, Mom." Panic laced his voice, and he turned and muffled his words into her shoulder. "I was just so mad. And Jarvis heard me railing about you and Max and said he had an idea for revenge. I didn't really think—"

Emma shushed him, running her fingers through his golden-blond hair. "It's okay, Cody. We'll work this out." She wrapped her arms around him. "This isn't your fault. You didn't light the match."

Mama Jeanie and Ava came outside and stood on the porch, Mama Jeanie's face a mask of disbelief as she tucked Ava against her side. "I never."

Emma had never seen anything like it, either. She knew these teens came from troubled backgrounds—clearly—but to set fire to the camp, to try to hurt Max so intentionally when all he'd done was want the best for them…it broke her heart.

She could only imagine how he felt—and on top of the personal whammy she'd already handed him, no less. Guilt crept up her insides like the flames crept up the barn toward the roof.

"I've got him!" Brady came around the far side of the flaming building, Jarvis's arm caught in Brady's unyielding grip. "And his book of matches."

Max's lips pressed together in a firm line as he took the book from Brady. "Take him to his room please, and have Tim monitor him." He met Jarvis's gaze, which didn't hold for long as the boy lowered his eyes in defeat. "I'll deal with you—and your parents—later."

Jarvis shuffled off with Tim, but not before sending Cody a scalding glance. Cody met his gaze head-on and didn't back down—neither did he puff up, ready for a fight.

Emma leaned to whisper to him. "You did the right thing, telling Max—I mean, your dad—about the fire."

"I know." He shrugged a little, eyes still focused on Jarvis's back. "Doesn't make it easy."

"That's true." She watched Max step back as the firefighters arrived and took over the scene, took in his crestfallen expression as he stood with his hands resting on top of his head. "Right is rarely easy, baby."

* * *

Hours later, Max and Emma sat under the star-lit sky on the porch, surrounded by leftover plastic cups of cider, remnants of chocolate chip cookies and the lingering scent of smoke. The fire, while contained to one portion of the barn thanks to the quick discovery and the prompt arrival of the fire department, only did minimal damage. The campers had all gone to bed for the night, way past their scheduled time, with grim faces. Jarvis's family had taken him home a little while ago, juvenile detention the next stop on his particular journey. It seemed the teen's choices had shaken them all up, especially Katie, who came to Emma after the chaos had dimmed.

"I have a confession," she'd whispered, her red hair dusted with ash that continued to float from the barn roof. "I haven't been honest with Max."

She'd gone on to admit that she'd been a part of a gang back home for years and couldn't get out. She'd gotten busted initially for repeated shoplifting, which was what sent her to Camp Hope in the first place—but only after she intentionally shoplifted all the more, hoping to be sent away to safety.

"I can't carry the secret anymore, Miss Emma. Not after watching Jarvis do something so stupid. I mean, if he reaches his limit and tries to burn down a barn, what am I capable of? I don't want to break." She'd looked so scared and so young that Emma had gathered her in a hug and assured her that the truth was always best. She'd stood by her side while Katie told Max, and he'd promised her an extra-long One4One session the next morning where they'd set everything straight and look into long-term options to keep her safe.

"This day has been unreal." She leaned her head back against the porch swing beside Max. "Tonya leaving. Cody's discovery and breakthrough. Jarvis's freak-out. Katie's confession."

"So many secrets." Max rocked their swing in a gentle rhythm. "You were right about Jarvis. I'm sorry I didn't heed your advice sooner. We both knew all along something was too good to be true about Katie, though, didn't we?"

"Yeah. I think she was so relieved to be free of her past, she didn't care what the camp was like." Emma shook her head. "She was just grateful to be away from that gang. But didn't stop to think about what would happen when she had to go home."

"They can't stay here forever. Guess there's several important calls to make tomorrow." Max pushed them slightly higher on the swing, and a smoky breeze wafted through Emma's hair. "Funny how secrets always seem a good idea at the time...." His voice trailed off, and she didn't know if he were being sincere or taking a well-justified jab at her.

"I think it's best if I take Cody back to Texas." Her statement planted Max's feet on the ground, and the swing came to an abrupt stop. "I can plead with the judge for a different facility, explain the conflict of interest or whatever. Maybe they'll have pity. This is just too much." Her voice broke. "Too much on all of us."

Especially on her, if she were being selfish and painfully honest. How could she keep working at the camp, or even keep Cody there at all, when their family dynamics were so tangled no one could sort them out? Her heart broke over and over just being in Max's presence, knowing he'd never be able to forgive to the point that she desired. To the point of their being a family.

"That's crazy." Max finally spoke, breaking the silence of the night. "He needs his family."

"But you're here. And I'm there."

"That could change." Max lifted his eyebrow at Emma, and her hopes hitched before she remembered Caley's comment alluding to obligation. No. That wasn't best for anyone, especially not Cody. They'd made it this far on their own. She and Max could work out some kind of custody arrangement, but when it came to being a family...they couldn't force that. Not even for Cody's sake.

"How could you even say that?" She twisted on the swing to face Max. "I know you're going to forgive me, eventually, but that doesn't mean you have to take us on."

"I already have forgiven you." He took her hand and ran his finger over the creases of her knuckles. "I forgave you this afternoon, when we were searching for Cody. I probably forgave you even sooner than that." He shook his head. "But I need you to forgive me."

She blinked in disbelief. "For what? I'm the one who lied to you, and our son, for years."

"I judged you."

She waited for his explanation, slowly pushing the swing into motion once more.

"I didn't hear you out and made my own assumptions. When you finally got to tell me what really happened, it made sense, Emma. Made me wonder if maybe I'd have done the same. You were thinking of Cody." He lifted one shoulder in a shrug, identical to Cody's. "I was still making bad choices, just in taking the deal even if I didn't use the drugs that time." He sighed. "We're all paying for the past here, and I think it's time we stop. Move forward in God's forgiveness."

It sounded too good to be true. Emma squeezed his hand, wondering if this would be the last time she'd get to hold it. "I don't know what to say."

"I do." Cody's voice sounded from the open front door, and Emma jerked, rocking the swing to a stop. She'd almost forgotten he'd been assigned to clean up the inside of the house for Mama Jeanie and do the dishes left over from the search crew. "Tell him we want to stay, Mom."

He came on the porch and stood before the swing. Emma scooted over, and he plopped down in the middle. "I don't want to go back to Texas.

It's—it's no good for me." He rubbed his palms over his jeans. "I feel different here. I don't want to get sucked back in."

Emma looked at Max over the top of Cody's head, and he nodded slowly, catching her urgent point. "Cody." He waited until Cody met his eyes. "It's good to get away from reality sometimes and learn new things. Sort of figure out who we are."

Cody nodded eagerly.

"But at some point, you have to live in the real world again. Put what you learned and believed into action."

His shoulders slumped. "So does that mean we have to go back to Dallas?"

"I think you should finish the session here, at least. There's not even two weeks left, and we have that big Thanksgiving meal coming up Thursday." Max jostled him in the ribs. "I bet there's room in there for some of Mama Jeanie's famous Cajun turkey."

"Mom?" Cody's pleading expression tugged at her heart.

She nodded slowly. "I think Max is right. Let's finish the camp and go from there."

"From there?" He frowned. "But—"

Max raised his eyebrows at Cody, and he stopped midsentence and sighed. "Yes, ma'am."

Talk about unexpected blessings. Emma couldn't ignore the warmth seeping through her heart at the way Max took over in such a natural way. He was going to be a great dad.

But dad didn't always equal husband.

There was the hollow ache again.

"Why don't you take this trash inside, and then I'll take you to the dorm. It's way past bedtime." Max waited until Cody had gathered the remaining debris and taken it inside the house before pulling Emma to stand beside him. "I let you walk away once before, Emma Shaver, and I'm not making that mistake again."

Her heart stammered in her chest, and the ache began to narrow into something almost manageable. Was this even possible?

"I should have followed you when you left the first time."

She was afraid to hope. He regretted not following her the first time? But why? She had to know. "Because it was the right thing to do?"

"No." He snorted. "Did anything I did back then seem like it was based on the right thing to do?"

So much she could say there. She just shook her head.

"I wanted you back. I loved you, Emma. But my immature pride and stubbornness wouldn't let me. I thought if you rejected me, then I shouldn't have to chase you." He leaned forward and pressed his cheek against hers. "Don't make me chase you, Emma. I'm really pretty busy around here."

She hiccupped back a laugh of surprise. "Is that

so?" The tease broke the weight around her heart and set it free. No obligation. Just her. Just him. Cody.

And love.

"We're not kids anymore. Let's give this a real try, whatever it takes. I love you, Emma." His lips were a breath apart from hers, and she found herself stretching on her toes to brush them with her own.

"I love you, too. Always have." She hugged him back, heart soaring, and knew he had to feel it thumping against the pocket of his shirt. She closed her eyes, nestling against the familiarity of his embrace. God had brought them full circle—despite their failures, their sin, their mistakes—He'd worked all things for good. Just like He promised.

And the best part was His forgiveness covered it all.

"You always have, huh? And always will?" The confidence in Max's gaze spoke a contradiction to the question. He already knew the answer.

"Just try to get rid of me again." She grinned at his responding chuckle. There was still a lot to figure out, a lot to wade through. But by the grace of God, they'd get there—all three of them. Because God knew from the beginning, secret son or not, they were meant to be a forever family.

Epilogue

"Mama Jeanie, you've outdone yourself again." Max settled in his chair at the head of the table, breathing in the aroma of walnut-crusted turkey, green bean casserole and honey-buttered rolls— to name a few. The table seemed almost unable to bear the load of the food and serving dishes covering every square inch.

He could relate. He knew a little something about carrying burdens. He shot a glance to his right, where Emma was trying to convince Cody that the sweet potato casserole tasted great even though it was orange, and smiled, a swell of thankfulness rising in his heart. Across from the two of them, Brady, Caley and Ava sat in a row, Caley and Ava giggling more like sisters than stepmother-daughter as they bent their heads over their plates.

"Thank you, but I had help this year, my boy." Mama Jeanie grinned down the length of table at him as she plucked her napkin from the decorative ring and placed it in her lap. "Your new wife there knows her way around a kitchen."

And his heart.

"You know that turkey was all you, Mama Jeanie. Don't give me too much credit. I pretty much heated and reheated." She gestured to the counter in the kitchen where an assortment of desserts waited. "Though I confess to making the pies. All four different kinds."

"Mmm. My kind of woman." Max nudged Emma's leg under the table with his boot, and the sassy wink she shot him warmed his skin. He still couldn't believe how much had happened in a year. In fact, it was worth announcing out loud.

He stood, tapping his knife lightly on his glass of water—real glass, which didn't happen often at Camp Hope, where all things plastic and sensible reigned. But today was worth celebrating—their first Thanksgiving as a whole family.

"I'd like to make a toast." He smiled at Emma, then at her mom, who sat on the other side of Cody, then at Mama Jeanie, his friends and finally at his son. "Every Thanksgiving at Camp Hope, we've made it a tradition to go around the table and voice what we're thankful for. This year, we didn't schedule a camp over the holiday, but I'd still like to keep up the tradition. So I'll go first."

He cleared his throat, knowing Brady would never let him hear the end of it if he teared up, then decided it really didn't matter. Men who discovered they had a secret son and then rediscovered love with the woman of their dreams could shed a manly tear or two. "This has been a crazy year, but one of the best. I wouldn't trade a single moment, however rocky they might have been at first." He reached over and rested his hand on Emma's shoulder. "This year, I'm thankful for second chances. For love and family."

Emma squeezed his hand as he sat down, then brushed her hair back from her face and gave that shy smile she always did when she spoke in front of a group—the same smile she'd offered to countless teen girls in the past year as she led beside him at the camp. "I'm thankful for hope. That just like God, it's always nearby, even when we can't necessarily feel it."

Everyone looked at Cody to go next. He stopped midchew and tried to hide a roll in his lap. "Do I have to?" He turned pleading eyes to his mom, who nodded. With a sigh, he put his roll on his plate and fisted his napkin in both hands. His voice rang timid, but sincere. "I'm thankful for a lot of stuff. For moving this year and getting away from those old friends of mine and making new ones here. And for finding my dad." He looked at Max, then away, and Max's heart thumped double in his chest. "I wish we had sooner. But I'm learning at church that everything happens for a reason, and I'm just happy we're all together now." Then Cody grinned, the same grin Max had seen in a mirror growing up in his own teen years. "And I'm really thankful that there's four kinds of pie."

Everyone laughed, breaking the band of emotion that tightened Max's throat, and he pointed at his new mother-in-law in relief. "Next."

She patted Cody's shoulder and reached around him to rub Emma's arm. "I'm thankful that all my family is back in one place. And for new additions." She winked at Max.

Mama Jeanie folded her hands atop her empty plate as she took her turn. "I'm thankful for the lot of you. All such good friends and family, taking care of each other and looking out for each other. It's a blessing to watch." She pointed at every person around the table. "And never forget the hand of the Good Lord is on you all. That's something to be thankful about right there."

Caley murmured her agreement, as she and Ava took turns announcing their blessings. Then Brady wrapped it up. "I'm thankful for family, friends and the chance to celebrate together." He reached over and tapped Max's arm. "And thankful that nothing is impossible with God—not even changing the most stubborn of hearts."

"Hey, I'd argue, but...we all know it's true." He grinned at his friend. "And while we're being sappy, I'll admit I'm thankful that God uses the most unlikely people in our lives to get through to us."

"Now I'm unlikely?" Brady scowled, a tease in his eyes.

Emma snorted. "I think he meant me."

"That's probably true of all of us." Caley laughed. "On that note, Max, why don't you say grace already so we can eat?"

"Great idea. Let's pray." As Max bowed his head to bless the meal, he couldn't resist one more glance around the table, one full of food, family, friends—and love. His gaze lingered on Cody, then on Emma, who opened one eye to check on him as he knew she would. Their gazes met and mingled, and the love he saw returned in her eyes was one of the biggest blessings of all.

"Happy Thanksgiving." She mouthed the words to him, and he mouthed it back.

Thankful, indeed.

* * * * *

Dear Reader,

Sometimes, life throws curveballs that don't just knock you off balance; they knock you flat on your back in the dirt. That's what happened to me during the writing of this novel, and it's what happened to Max when he discovered the truth about Cody.

I've seen over the course of my life that people—both real and fictional—have a choice to make when they get bowled over. They can either stay down, complain about the dirt while wallowing in it and carry grudges toward the one who threw the ball (or toward the One who allowed it to be thrown) or, they can get up, brush off and turn their wounds over to the One who always keeps His promises. The One whose love is everlasting. The One who died for us—Jesus Christ.

As Max discovers in this story, secrets can be devastating—but nothing is too hard for God to work for the good of those who love Him, as is promised to us in Romans 8:28.

Whether you're walking along just fine, or whether you're suddenly gazing up at the sky, wondering what happened and why you're covered in dirt, you have a choice to make. To follow God, or not. To believe in His truth, or not. To allow Him to work *all* things for good, or not.

Max made the right decision. I hope you will, too.

Sincerely,

Betsy St. Amant

Questions for Discussion

1. Emma carried a heavy secret for the majority of her adult life. Have you ever kept a secret that weighed on you nonstop? Do you think secrets in general are good, bad or somewhere in between?

2. Do you think Emma's choice to keep Cody's father's identity a secret from her parents was a good one or bad one?

3. Max had a past he wasn't proud of, but that past enabled him to reach out to teens because he could relate to them. How is this an example of Romans 8:28 coming to life?

4. Emma dated Max in high school because of temporary rebellion against her parents. Have you ever grown tired of being "the good girl" all the time? Did you ever act out in a similar way?

5. Do you think Emma's fear that Cody had inherited Max's "bad boy" genes was merited or a myth? Do you think a heritage like that is left in one's DNA?

6. Cody made bad choices and got into trouble because of wanting to be accepted and receive attention he felt he didn't receive elsewhere.

Why do you think kids and teenagers struggle with the concept that negative attention is better than none at all? Do you think adults are tempted to feel the same?

7. Max's best friend, Brady, played a key role in his turning from his wayward life and finding the right path toward God. Have you ever had someone play that role in your life in a spiritual or emotionally positive way? Did you ever thank them?

8. Emma's relationship with her mom was strained because of her secret and because of misplaced judgments on both sides. Has a secret ever strained a friendship or relationship in your life? How did you handle it?

9. Max and Emma struggled to get beyond the weight of the past in different ways regarding their relationship with each other. Why was forgiveness needed on both sides?

10. Many of the teens at Camp Hope carried one secret or another. What was Tonya's secret, and what do you think happened to her after she left the camp?

11. Katie's secret was perhaps the most surprising of all because she was the most adept at carry-

ing it. Have you ever been shocked to discover the truth about someone's life or background? How can you help someone in that position?

12. Jarvis is an example of how some teens might never discover the desire to turn to the right path in life, despite being given every opportunity spiritually, emotionally, mentally and physically. Do you think a person ever reaches the point of "too late," or do you believe that God's grace offers endless second chances?

13. Do you ever struggle with receiving forgiveness like Emma did at the end of the story? Do you struggle more with extending forgiveness?

14. Emma and Max were able to overcome their differences and the past by the grace of God and by the mutual effort of forgiveness and desire to make their family a permanent one. Have you ever experienced such love and sacrifice in your own life?

LARGER-PRINT BOOKS!

GET 2 FREE
LARGER-PRINT NOVELS
PLUS 2 FREE
MYSTERY GIFTS

Love Inspired®
SUSPENSE
RIVETING INSPIRATIONAL ROMANCE

Larger-print novels are now available...